FIRE IN THE BLOOD

A BILLIONAIRE SINGLE DADDY ROMANCE - THEIR SECRET DESIRE BOOK TWO

MICHELLE LOVE

MEGAN LEE

CONTENTS

Blurb   v

1. Chapter One - Praying   1
2. Chapter Two – Waiting Game   9
3. Chapter Three – Dreaming with a Broken Heart   18
4. Chapter Four – Hello   26
5. Chapter Five – My Blood   34
6. Chapter Six – Seven Devils   42
7. Chapter Seven – I Wanna Be Yours   52
8. Chapter Eight – It's Definitely You   65
9. Chapter Nine – Stressed Out   76
10. Chapter Ten – Make Me Feel   88
11. Chapter Eleven – Breathe   98
12. Chapter Twelve – Humble   110
13. Chapter Thirteen – Wires   116
14. Chapter Fourteen – Song to the Siren   129
15. Chapter Fifteen – What Kind of Man?   139
16. Chapter Sixteen – So Far Away   149
17. Chapter Seventeen – Wherever I Go   156
18. Chapter Eighteen – Never Be The Same   165
19. Chapter Nineteen – Take Me Home   174
20. Chapter Twenty – Am I Wrong   187
21. Chapter Twenty-One – Big Girls Cry   198
22. Chapter Twenty-Two – All Night   208
23. Chapter Twenty-Three – House of Cards   215
24. Chapter Twenty-Four – Faded   224
25. Chapter Twenty-Five – Across the Universe   231

Sneak Peek - Chapter one Everything Changes   239

Made in "The United States" by:

Michelle Love & Megan Lee

© Copyright 2020

ISBN: 9781087860220

ALL RIGHTS RESERVED. No part of this publication may be reproduced or transmitted in any form whatsoever, electronic, or mechanical, including photocopying, recording, or by any informational storage or retrieval system without express written, dated and signed permission from the author

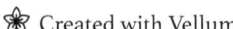 Created with Vellum

BLURB

Entertainment lawyer Jess Olden is single again after a break-up and ready to meet someone new, but when her best friend singer India Blue is seriously injured, Jess's own life is put on hold as she waits to hear if her best friend will survive.

Losing her concentration at work means she misses out on the biggest divorce case Hollywood has seen in years.

Movie star Teddy Hood has left his wife of six years, Dorcas Prettyman, and she's intent on making his life hell. Teddy approaches Jess, seeking the best lawyer out there, but distracted by her personal life, Jess turns him down and then watches as his reputation and life is destroyed by his ex.

When India pulls through and starts recovery, Jess returns her focus to her work and feels guilty for what happened to Teddy Hood. Determined to right a wrong, she contacts him and offers to help him regain custody of his young daughter. At first, he is resistant, too damaged by his legal and personal ordeal, but when they meet, there is an immediate attraction.

Trying to remain professional is difficult for them both, and soon Teddy and Jess are falling into a red-hot sexual relationship that leaves wanting more.

However, Dorcas is not a woman to be messed with, and soon she is making life hell for Jess and Teddy in more ways than one. Will the two lovers finally be able to love freely, and will Teddy ever get custody of his daughter? When Dorcas crosses a line, more than just love is put at risk as she makes it clear that she will never, ever let Teddy find happiness again…

Jess

Nothing mattered to me more in the last year than putting the man who tried to kill my best friend in jail.
Nothing.
So, when Hollywood star Teddy Hood asked me to represent him in his child custody battle, I had to turn him down.
Now, a year later, I've never regretted anything more.
Teddy Hood is angry, hurt… and sexy as all hell.
The trouble is he hates me.
The trouble is I can't stop thinking about him.

I have to get him to forgive me and I'll do anything to make that happen.

Because I need him in my life... and in my bed.

I want to feel his skin next to mine, his mouth on my body, his kiss on my lips...

I just have to get him to talk to me first and that...

That's going to be the hardest thing in the world...

Teddy

She turned me down a year ago and now I've lost custody of my kid, maybe forever.

I hate Jessica Olden and I don't care that it's not fair to blame her...

...but I do.

But it drives me mad that I can't get her out of my head: her big beautiful eyes, her dark hair, that perfect pink, pouty mouth...

Jess Olden is the most beautiful woman I've ever seen in my life, and I'm one of Hollywood's biggest stars—hey, I could have any woman I want.

Any woman.

But the one I want is the one I don't want.

I need to get her out of my head...

...it just won't be easy...

CHAPTER ONE - PRAYING

*M*anhattan

JESS OLDEN IGNORED her phone and waited for Margot to arrive at the restaurant. She hated this, hated it every time she broke up with a boyfriend or girlfriend, but this one was a particularly painful split. For a while there, she had thought Margot was the one: smart, funny, successful.

They had planned a future together without ever discussing whether they actually wanted the same things, and when Margot had tearfully confessed to Jess that she wanted the whole white picket fence and two-point-five kids thing, Jess knew it was over.

Not that she had any problem with that dream—it just wasn't for her. She hated the idea of marriage, and she'd never wanted kids. Something to do with her own upbringing...

"Hey, gorgeous." Margot was standing by her elbow when Jess looked around.

Margot's eyes were soft and sad, and as Jess stood to kiss her hello, they hugged for a beat too long. Finally, both silent with emotion, they sat and ordered, sitting quietly until the waiter brought them their wine.

Margot reached across the table and interlaced her fingers with Jess's. "I keep waking up in the night thinking this is a mistake. Maybe I was wrong; maybe it was just panic that made me say those things."

Jess smiled, but gently removed her hand. "We both know it wasn't, baby. It wasn't. It hurts like to hell to admit it, but..."

"God, Jess..."

"I know."

Neither of them ate much; they lightly talked around the fact that they were in pain, but towards the end of the meal, Margot's shoulders slumped, and she nodded. "You're right. We want different things."

"We do." Jess wasn't someone who cried, especially not in public, but she felt her eyes fill. "But I do love you, Margie. Never forget that."

"I love you, too." Margot's voice cracked, and she looked down as Jess's phone began to ring incessantly. "Answer that. It's driving me crazy."

Jess touched her hand as she answered the call. "Yes?"

"Jessie?"

"Lazlo?" She was immediately alert. Lazlo never called this late unless it was something serious. At first, she couldn't understand him, he was sobbing so hard, then when she caught the words 'Carter' and 'India' and worse still, 'stabbed,' her entire body went cold. "Lazlo, breathe. Tell me."

"She went to LeFevre; that's where she was hiding out. We think he was in league with Carter. Carter took her, Jess. We just found her. He stabbed her, again, Jess! Again!"

The breath froze in her lungs. "Is she..." *Please God, no, please don't let her be dead...*

"No. They're flying her to Lennox Hill now, but she's in bad shape. We're in another chopper on the way."

"I'll meet you there."

Margot looked up as Jess stood. "What is it, babe?"

"It's India. Carter caught up with her. She's hurt." Jess felt her throat close as the shock of what had happened hit her. Margot caught her as her knees gave way. "Come on. I'll drive you."

THEY ARRIVED at the hospital before the helicopter carrying India, and they had to wait around while the place was being locked down by the FBI and Lazlo's security team. Jess overheard the doctor saying the helicopter had arrived, and before anyone could stop her, she took the elevator to the roof.

They were rolling the gurney over to the lift just as she arrived, and Jess couldn't help her cry of distress when she saw her friend. India was covered in blood, deathly pale and unconscious. "Indy!" Jess darted to her friend's side as the paramedics shot her an annoyed look.

"She's my friend," she stuttered, resisting them from trying to push her aside. She grasped India's cold hand as they hurried into the elevator.

"We're taking her straight to surgery." One of the nurses took pity on the distraught woman. "We can't stop the bleeding."

The sheet covering India's abdomen was soaked with blood, and Jess clutched her hand tighter. "You have to fight, Indy, fight! Live! Don't let him win, please."

"Ma'am, please step aside now. We need to get her to surgery."

IN A DAZE, Jess let go of India's hand as they arrived on the surgical floor, and she slowly followed the gurney out until she could no longer move. Margot found her standing stock-still, staring into space, and steered her into the relatives' waiting room.

Jess had pulled herself together by the time Lazlo and India's lover, Massimo, arrived at the hospital. She quickly told them what she had discovered, leaving out the most gruesome parts.

"He did it," Massimo kept repeating, a man in total shock.

Lazlo was pale and Jess hugged him. "We have to be

positive." She took a deep breath in. "What happened to Carter?"

"She killed him."

"Oh, thank God." Jess felt her body relax. Braydon Carter had relentlessly stalked India after she survived his rape and stabbing and the murder of her mother in front of her twelve years prior. A few days previous to today's horror, he had shot one of India's closest friends, a sweet young kid called Sun, who was still recovering in a hospital in Seoul.

Jess rubbed her eyes. "Listen, I hate to be the practical one at a time like this, but we need to get ahead of this in the press. From what you told me, LeFevre is going to try and obfuscate responsibility as long as India is unconscious. I need to get a press statement ready."

"Jesus, Jess..."

"I know, but this is what we do, Laz, and you're in no fit state. Let me just check that they haven't got it already."

She flicked on the television in the waiting room and flicked to the news channels. To her relief, none had picked up the story yet; most of them were concerned with the newly announced divorce of movie stars Teddy Hood and Dorcas Prettyman, the Hollywood power couple for the last ten years. The divorce had come out of nowhere and mud was already being slung, mostly by Prettyman's team. Jess rolled her eyes. She'd had previous run-ins with Dorcas Prettyman and found her to be a vile attention seeker with little regard for anyone else.

Hood she didn't know, but she already had no

sympathy for anyone voluntarily involved themselves with Dorcas. Jess flicked off the television and went to work.

AN HOUR LATER, she saw the press gathering at the hospital entrance. She and Lazlo wrote a short statement, and Jess went down to read it, glaring at the surrounding journalists.

"Earlier this evening, India Blue was abducted by Braydon Carter, the man who twelve years ago attacked and seriously injured India and murdered her mother. During the ensuing struggle, Braydon Carter was killed, and India suffered serious abdominal injuries. She is currently in emergency surgery. We'll give you an update later, but in the meantime, we ask you respect both India's and her family's privacy and remember there are many other sick people and their families here who deserve their privacy as well. Thank you."

Jess ignored the flood of questions that exploded as soon as she finished speaking and went back into the hospital. *God.* She felt sick at this whole thing, mainly because of the inevitability of it all. Carter was always going to get to India, wasn't he? Obsession like that was unstoppable. Jess shivered. After her break-up with Margot, she could do with some serious alone-time, away from other people's shit. Not that Margot was ever toxic. She saw her approaching now and hugged her. "Thank you for being here, Margie. I don't know what I would have done."

Margot smiled at her. "You would have done just fine, my little tigress." She raised her hand to stroke Jess's face, then let it drop, realizing it was no longer appropriate to do. Jess felt a pang of sadness. Never again would she wake up to Margot's soft, gentle kiss.

"I should go now," Margot said, "give you all some privacy, but listen. Keep me up to date, right? And you need anything, anything, I'm here for you."

JESS WENT BACK UPSTAIRS after saying goodbye to Margot and found Massimo alone in the waiting room. He looked wrecked. "Lazlo has gone to make some phone calls. He got a message from Tae. The news has broken in Seoul. They're making the link between India and Sun's shooting, so this thing's gone international now."

"Any news from the surgeon?"

Massimo shook his head. "Not yet."

The television was flickering on the wall, the sound muted, and Jess watched as the news shifted from the Hood/Prettyman divorce to outside of Lennox Hill. She and Massimo watched her statement to the press, then it cut to a package of India performing and doing interviews. They also managed to rehash the Rome scandal, the nude photographs taken by a snoop paparazzi of India and Massimo making love. *So much for respecting India,* Jess thought grimly.

Massimo gave a choked laugh. "God, how beautiful does she look? Why would anyone want to destroy it?"

Jess put her hand on his shoulder. "Sick fucks will always be sick fucks, Massi. He's gone. He can't hurt her anymore."

Massimo nodded. "If she lives. Otherwise... he won."

"She *will* live," Jess said fiercely, hurt and anger in her voice. "There's no way India would give up now. Did you hear what she did to him? She wanted to live, Massi. For you, for Sun, for her Mom. For herself. She wanted to live. She's not going to give up now."

For the first time there was a faint smile on Massimo's handsome face. "Thank you. I needed to hear that."

"Look, why don't I go get us some coffee and maybe something to eat? We're no good to India if we collapse from hunger and thirst."

Jess patted his shoulder and went out of the room. She walked down the stairs to the cafeteria, hoping it was open this late, but as she came to the bottom of the stairwell, she stopped and bent double, trying to quell her sudden urge to scream, to cry, to indulge in everything her broken heart wanted to do. She sank to the floor, pulling her knees up to her chest and took several deep breaths. *Don't. Don't lose it now. This isn't about you.*

She took a deep lungful. India will live. Believe what you told Massimo.

"Yes," she said quietly to herself, "yes. She'll be fine. She'll be okay."

As she pulled herself to her feet, Jess told herself the same thing again and again, ignoring the simmering fear inside her that her friend might be too far gone this time.

2
CHAPTER TWO – WAITING GAME

L *os Angeles*

TEDDY HOOD STOOD in the empty house on Mulholland Drive and shook his head. Dorcas had finally agreed to selling their home, and now that she had finally moved her stuff out, the house was ready to be handed over to the new owner, an excited young actor who'd made his first million and wanted the now-legendary Hood/Prettyman mansion for himself.

Good. Let him have it. Teddy Hood was tired. Tired of the fighting, of the divorce, of Hollywood. Of Dorcas's spite.

He checked his watch. He would have to leave now to

get to his supervised visit time with his daughter, DJ. His mood lightened at the thought of seeing his darling tomboy daughter, only six and yet so headstrong. The only downside was…

Supervised visits. He swallowed the anger that the restriction riled in him. Damn you, Dorcas, and your lies. She'd made a big deal of his 'temper' to the press, and then to the custody judge who had been starstruck by her and had taken against Teddy. Unfairly, too, but Dorcas had the upper hand in the divorce and she knew it.

She knew way too much about Teddy's past. All of it: the early days of his acting career and what he had been put through. The stuff of nightmares and nothing he wanted out in the world. Nothing. And Dorcas had been gleeful when she told him that she would think nothing of revealing everything if she didn't come out as the 'winner' in their divorce.

He was just grateful she finally agreed to it. The face that the caring 'humanitarian' Dorcas Prettyman showed to the world was in sharp contrast to the destructive narcissist she actually was.

It had fooled him for a few years, too.

Teddy got into his car and drove across the city, glancing in the mirror to check he didn't look too grungy. He'd been growing his dark brown beard out, not to hipster lengths, but so it covered his handsome face enough that he felt as if he had a mask on. Of course, his brilliant cornflower blue eyes would always give him away, but that wasn't the point. He didn't want to be 'Teddy Hood,' pretty-boy movie star anymore... he wanted out of the game entirely.

No more Hollywood. God, what an appealing idea.

When he arrived at Dorcas's new 'rental,' a behemoth that was costing *him* nearly a quarter of a million a month, the supervisor greeted him and led him in. "We've had a bit of an upset," she whispered to him. The supervisor, Fliss, unlike the judge, had seen through Dorcas immediately and adored Teddy—not for his reputation, but for the way he was with DJ.

"What happened?"

"*Mommy* wanted DJ to wear a dress for some press photos. DJ had other ideas." Fliss, a non-nonsense middle-aged Englishwoman, tried to hide a grin. "Oh, DJ put on a dress but halfway through the photos, ripped it off. Underneath she had a *Never Mind the Bollocks* shirt on. Mommy wasn't pleased."

Teddy grinned widely. "How the hell did she get her hands on that?"

Fliss opened her eyes wide in innocence. "Can I help it if I leave my laptop open on Amazon.com?"

"You are a bad, bad influence. But thank you," he patted her back, laughing. "So, I take it Dorcas went into one of her screaming jags?"

"Yup. She's now in bed with one of her *heads*."

Teddy rolled his eyes in unison with Fliss. "Good."

In the living room, DJ looked up with pure joy as her

father entered the room and flew into his arms. She looked cheerful enough. "Did Fliss tell you?"

"She did. You are a bad, bad child, Dinah-Jane."

"Then why are you smiling, Daddy?" DJ grinned widely at him and threw her arms around his neck. "How long can you stay tonight?"

Teddy shot a look at Fliss who made a face. "Just the usual hour, Monkey."

DJ's face fell. "Oh."

Teddy hugged his daughter tightly. "It'll get better soon, I swear it will. In the meantime, let's not waste any time moping, hey?"

DJ rallied, smiled, and they played together for an hour, laughing and joking around.

Teddy hated saying goodbye; it was the only time DJ got teary, but tonight, she clung on even more. "Can't I come live with you, Daddy? I promise I'll be good."

Teddy's heart shattered. "Monkey, you don't know how much I wish you could. I wish, I wish, I wish you could."

He hated to leave her crying, but Dorcas was fierce about him leaving exactly on the hour. As he walked out of the mansion, he heard his ex-wife calling to him. Bunching his hands into fists to stop himself breaking down in front of her, he turned.

Dorcas Prettyman had always relied on her good looks for everything in life. The daughter of a screen legend herself, her path to stardom was also eased by her spectacular looks, silky dark hair, and silver eyes. When she had been younger, her body was the stuff of legend, Jessica-Rabbit curves, but once she had built a reputation not just as an actress but as a charity maven, she had simply stopped eating. Teddy also suspected she was using but could never find proof. Dorcas could run classes on how to hide a person's vices.

A title which, of all people, Dorcas Prettyman was least entitled. She would host benefits but would ask an extortionate fee to do it and insist on NDAs for everyone. Anyone that crossed her was met with a tsunami of spite so vicious it could leave someone speechless for days. She was, quite simply, terrifying.

And now in her mid-forties, her looks were starting to fade, her dark hair was now dyed an unflattering straw-blonde, and younger, prettier, easier to work with actresses were taking the roles she had always expected to be offered. Rather than move into character roles like her contemporaries, she began to write her own roles... which were *not* well-received. Dorcas had become a laughing-stock behind the scenes in Hollywood, and Teddy had borne the brunt of her rage.

She hadn't started to beat him until DJ was three years old. It was on the night of the Oscars and nominee Dorcas had been passed over for an actress she hated. The actress in question, Tiger Rose, had won Best Actress for a film starring opposite Teddy and their onscreen chemistry had been the talk of Hollywood.

Dorcas, of course, immediately suspected they had

been fucking, despite Teddy's denials. Unlike most Hollywood husbands, he had remained faithful, even through the last few years when any love between him and Dorcas had been minimal.

Teddy was dead on his feet, having taken a red-eye flight back from a film set in the Ukraine the previous day. He'd supported Dorcas on the red carpet, of course, and commiserated when she had lost. Of course, he had to applaud his costar for her own win, and that had set Dorcas off. In the limousine on the way home, she had practically screamed at him, blaming him for her loss.

He had gone to sleep in the guest room, eager to fend off any further argument, but in the early hours, he had been rocked awake by searing pain as Dorcas beat him with an empty vodka bottle. It smashed across his brow eventually, and Teddy had been left with a scar above his right eye.

It was all hushed up, of course, and Teddy declined to press charges for DJ's sake. Dorcas had been repentant... *that* time. She never made the mistake of hitting him where it showed again. Teddy, his male pride more than dented, made a show of putting up with her moods, never telling anyone how miserable he was, but inevitably, rumors started. A former nanny to DJ, whom Dorcas had verbally abused, broke her NDA and sold a story to the press of Dorcas's moods and how whipped Teddy was. Teddy was humiliated.

But it wasn't until his beloved younger brother Billy had been diagnosed with a terminal brain tumor did

Teddy see the light. As Billy wasted away in hospital, he begged his older brother, Teddy, not to waste any more time. "She's poison," Billy had said, his honesty forthright because he had nothing to lose. "She always has been. Teddy, please, take DJ and go. You'll both be happier."

Teddy told Dorcas he was leaving her the evening of Billy's funeral. She reacted as expected, laughing in his face, not taking him seriously.

She soon found out he was deadly serious and went into damage control mode. Nannies, bodyguards were all paid off to say he was a bad father and neglectful. Dorcas was clever—she never outright said he was abusive—that would be very hard to prove, because he was the farthest thing from it, but she started a whisper campaign. Going into one of her saintly martyr modes, she gave interviews where she would espouse how hard it was for a single mother out there, how she barely had time to shower because of it, that she cared little for the trappings of fame—all while renting a beautiful mansion and making Teddy pay for it.

TEDDY DROVE HOME NOW, his heart heavy at leaving DJ, and when he got to the small apartment he had rented—private, out of the way, and nowhere a movie star was expected to live—he took his jacket off and slumped onto the sofa. He flicked the news on, expecting to hear more about himself and Dorcas, but instead saw a beautiful woman speaking outside a hospital building, surrounded by press. He turned the television up.

"During the ensuing struggle, Braydon Carter was killed, and India suffered serious abdominal injuries. She is currently in emergency surgery. We'll give you an update later, but in the meantime, we ask you respect both India's and her family's privacy and remember there are many other sick people and their families here who deserve their privacy as well. Thank you."

Jesus. India Blue was hurt? Teddy felt a pang of sadness. He didn't know the singer well, had only met her a couple of times, but she was a sweetheart, a rare talent. Teddy watched as the spokeswoman walked back into the hospital. She looked tired and distressed, but still walked with purpose and with confidence. The reporter at the scene identified her as India's lawyer, Jess Olden.

Jess Olden… Teddy had definitely heard of her; in fact, she was legendary in Hollywood circles for winning the best possible outcomes for her clients in savage, bitter battles regarding alimony, property, and more importantly, custody.

An idea formed in his mind, but he put it aside for now. Jess Olden was clearly devastated by her friend's attempted murder, and now wouldn't be the ideal time to ask if she could take him on.

But when—and if—India Blue made it, and Teddy hoped she would, he would approach Jess Olden. Ask for her help.

Because he wanted his daughter back for more than a

supervised hour every two days, and he had the strangest idea that Jess Olden was the right person to help him.

And it had nothing, nothing at all to do with the fact that she was the most beautiful woman he had ever seen.

Nothing.

CHAPTER THREE – DREAMING WITH A BROKEN HEART

ew York

Jess didn't cry until Lazlo told her that India was awake, that her beloved friend was going to make it. Then, glad to be alone in her apartment, she was able to bawl, to sob out her utter relief. She let all her emotions out, finally hiccupping to a halt and cranking on the shower. She let the water run down her body for longer than usual, hoping to ease some of the muscle ache.

After drying her hair and dressing, she grimaced as she glanced into the mirror. Her dark hazel eyes were puffy, thick violet circles underneath them, and her usually glowing skin was wan.

"Nope, not a good look." She decided she would work

from home today before going to the hospital. Lazlo had told her that although India was awake, she was exhausted, unsurprisingly, and that the doctor had advised no more than two visitors at a time. Jess knew India would want her brother and her lover with her, so she agreed to provide relief later. She couldn't wait to hold her friend though.

Lazlo also told her that India had positively identified her politician father as the one who had instigated her attempted murder, and Jess went into work mode, contacting the police and finding out what charges were being brought against Philip LeFevre. She also wanted to make absolutely sure that India would not face any charges for killing Braydon Carter, the man who had been so obsessed with her that he had almost killed her twice.

The District Attorney reassured her. "It was self-defense, pure and simple. There will be no charges filed against India, I can assure you. As for LeFevre, at least one count of murder for India's mother, three counts of attempted murder, but really, Jess, I could be here for hours reciting what we're going to charge that son-of-a-bitch with. He's going away forever."

"To think he almost ran for president."

The DA had laughed humorlessly. "I'd say he would have never gotten in, but apparently, right now, anything goes."

"Right? What a world."

Jess called her Los Angeles office to update them on India's condition, smiling when she heard their relief.

"There's a long way to go yet, but it's good news." She heard her assistant, Bee, relay the news to the others in the office and heard their cries of delight. There was a reason India was so popular both with her fans and those she worked with.

Jess smiled. "Listen, I'm going to be here in New York for the foreseeable future. I'm going to help the DA send Philip LeFevre down, so as of now, no new clients whoever they might be. We will, of course, keep working with our existing client list, and I'll fly back and forth, but as I say, no newbies."

"Sure thing, boss. Give our love to India when you see her, won't you?"

Jess smiled. "Of course. Thanks, Bee."

She snagged her laptop from the bedroom and sat down to work, keeping half an eye on the television news in case anything leaked about India that they didn't want out there.

Since the news that India was awake was made public, the ardor outside the hospital had died down a little, but it didn't stop some of the more gutter-like press from trying to get in to see her. Jess smirked when she remembered Massimo, half-crazed with grief, discovering a *pap* hovering outside the door of India's room. The whole floor knew of Massimo's anger that day. Jess wondered how he was coping.

She picked up the phone and made a call. In Seoul, Tae picked up and greeted her, sounding more cheerful than for a while. "Hi, Jessie."

"Hey, Tae. How's Sun?"

"Comparing scars with another patient at the moment—it's the cutest thing. Well, if seeing your lover with a hole in his chest can be described as cute." His breath hitched a little, and Jess could tell he was trying to keep from screaming at that thought. He rallied and chuckled softly. "Honestly, nothing can keep this little angel down. How's Indy?"

"I think if she were with Sun right now, they would be comparing scars. Tae, I think it's just their way of being happy to be alive. I know it must be hard to hear the morgue humor."

"A little, but I'm just glad he's here to make bad jokes. Listen, I'd like to call Indy, but I don't want to intrude. How're Massi and Lazlo holding up?"

"Exhausted but relieved."

"And you?"

"Same."

Tae sighed. "When they're well... we have to all get together."

"I agree, honey. Listen, Tae... it's over. They're hurt, yes, but they made it. Carter is dead. It's over."

THE CONVERSATION WAS on her mind later, when she'd replied to every important email she had, deleted the rest, and gone to the kitchen to make herself a snack. *Family.* That's what they were, despite the distance in geography, despite the cultural differences, despite everything. In this industry, Jess thought, there are so many fake relationships, lavender marriages, PR romances, false friends. But not them. *Not us*, she thought, *not us.* The love between all of them was real, palpable... forever.

But Jess also felt lonely, seeing the love between India and Massimo, and Sun and Tae. Oh, to have that perfect love. Not that she believed in it, most of the time, but her four friends were the most convincing evidence she had ever seen. To find that one person who fit you exactly.

It would be nice, Jess thought, taking her cup of tea back to the couch as she waited for her pasta to cook. *Nice, but not necessary. Right?*

She pushed the thought away. Too much was happening for her to lose focus now. She glanced at the television and grimaced. Dorcas Prettyman was simpering as she was being awarded a star on the Hollywood Boulevard. *Yeah, we know you paid for that, bitch.* Jess's lip curled as she watched the overly-exaggerated mannerisms of the other woman.

"Stupid woman thinks she's Grace Kelly," Jess muttered to herself. The screen cut to a shot of Prettyman with Teddy Hood, who looked miserable. Dude's gorgeous, Jess thought, but what the hell was he doing with her? *Good move divorcing the spider, man.*

She didn't listen to the rest of the segment, but Teddy Hood's blue eyes haunted her. That was misery right there. Poor guy. Distracted, she looked him up. He was five years younger than his soon-to-be-ex-wife, forty to her forty-five. A successful actor in his own right and had quietly built his own resume with small, independent parts before marrying Dorcas and being propelled into the big time. He didn't seem the type to do Oscar-bait-ey films, happy to play character parts and take second or third billing, but he constantly garnered good reviews and had been nominated for some minor awards, even winning a few.

What on earth did you get out of this marriage? Jess's interest was piqued then, and instead of concentrating on her own work, she did some research into the Hood/Prettyman marriage until Lazlo called her and asked her to come back to the hospital.

Los Angeles

Teddy arrived at Dorcas's home a little early but didn't wait for the appointed time to be buzzed in. Expecting to see Fliss, he was taken aback to see a new woman coming toward him. She didn't smile. "Mr. Hood. You're early."

He pointedly checked his watch. "By about two minutes. Where's Fliss?"

"Ms. Chambers has been replaced at the request of Ms. Prettyman. She felt the young lady was not a good influence on Dinah-Jane."

Teddy clenched his jaw in irritation. "And why was I not informed or consulted?"

Was he imagining it or was there a slight smirk on the

woman's face? "You would have to ask Ms. Prettyman." She mimicked him checking his watch. "You can see your daughter now."

DJ WAS QUIET, subdued and Teddy could tell she was upset about Fliss. "Why did Fliss have to go away, Daddy?"

"I don't know, sweetie, but I'll be asking Mommy."

DJ's eyes slid away from his at the mention of her mother, and suddenly Teddy's heart clenched. He shot a look at the supervisor. "Monkey… is anything wrong?"

DJ shook her head, cutting her eyes at the stranger, and Teddy knew she didn't want to say anything in front of her lest it get back to Dorcas. He was haunted by the same thought again. God, please… not that…

Was Dorcas abusing DJ? Was she taking her anger out on her child? Teddy held her tightly. He couldn't ask her in front of the supervisor, nor could he examine his daughter for bruises. "Sweetie…" He made her look at him. "You know you can tell me anything, right? Anything?"

"I know." The way her voice quivered made his heart shatter. DJ hugged him tightly.

It was a somber hour together, and Teddy had to fight back tears leaving her behind. Dorcas hadn't made an appearance, wisely avoiding the anger he felt like unleashing on her. Strange. Usually she would use that to smear his character further, especially if she had witnesses.

It was only after he'd gotten home that he found it. He

pulled the screwed-up piece of paper from his pocket and opened it. His already fractured heart gave another crack as he read the childish scrawl.

"Daddy, please help me. Mommy is angry all the time."

"Oh, God..." Without thinking, he snagged his cellphone and called his agent, asking for the phone number he needed now.

When she'd given it to him, he didn't wait, dialing the cellphone number. When the call was picked up, he didn't bother with hellos. "God, please... this is Teddy Hood... you have to help me..."

CHAPTER FOUR – HELLO

Los Angeles

ONE YEAR LATER...

JESS STRETCHED out her limbs and glanced out of the window. Christmas Eve and it was still eighty degrees in Southern California. She laughed to herself and got out of bed, hearing voices in the kitchen of her condo.

"You fiends had better not be eating all my food," she called out as she tugged her robe around her and padded down the hallway. In her kitchen, four very guilty faces grinned back at her, and she laughed, rolling her eyes.

"We didn't eat much," India said with a smirk. She was perched on Massimo's knees, her arm around his neck. She was still recovering and was thinner than her usual curvy weight, but the color had started to come back into her skin now, and the relief of knowing she was finally safe also played a part. Massimo looked like a man wiped out by love as he cradled her in his arms.

Their friends, Alex and Coco, best friends but not lovers—Alex was gay—were busy flipping pancakes onto plates. Coco was pregnant... with Alex's baby. They had both wanted kids for so long, but when Coco found out she had very little chance of conceiving and that the chance was rapidly decreasing as she entered her late thirties, Alex had offered to father a child with her through IVF. After the second try, they'd gotten pregnant and were both so excited about the baby, they could hardly wait.

Jess had dated a few people since Margot, but nothing had stuck. She'd been concentrating so much on putting Philip LeFevre behind bars for what he had done to India that nothing else had mattered.

Now that he was in prison for the rest of his life, she felt like a weight had been lifted. Time to get some space—to enjoy life. Hence, inviting her friends for Christmas. Tonight, they would all attend a party thrown by one of Jess's clients, Cole Henning, an actor hoping for his first Oscar nomination the following January.

Until then, the friends sat around playing games, eating, being with each other, and talking about the future.

India and Massimo were planning their wedding for the following May, a double wedding with Sun and Tae, and Jess listened as they excitedly told them the plans for their special day.

Coco and Alex talked about their child due in the summer, and how it would work between them. "We're going to live together for as long as it both woks for us," Alex explained, his hand resting on Coco's back. "If either of us feel we need space... we'll work something else out, but this kid is going to be the most loved ever."

"I don't doubt it," Jess said, smiling at them both. She looked over at India, catching her and Massimo sharing a long look, a brief kiss. "Don't tell me you're broody, too?"

India laughed, but Jess noticed the slight catch in her voice. "Not yet. I'm selfish enough that I don't want to share Massi for a while." India smiled a little. "And to be honest..." She shared another loaded glance with Massi. "We don't know yet if I'll be able to carry a child. The knife... it damaged my uterus. They were able to repair it, and the docs tell me a pregnancy could go ahead, but no one really knows until we try. So..."

"...so, we're waiting. Until India has fully healed. Until we're ready to try." Massi stroked his love's face tenderly. "And we're going to explore every option, right? So, there's no pressure."

India smiled at him gratefully, and Jess felt again the pang of longing she always felt around them. *Nope. You're a strong, independent woman. You don't need anyone.*

. . .

LATER, they took a cab to the party in the Hollywood Hills. Cole himself came to greet them, handing out flutes of champagne—and fruit juice to a sulky Coco—before leading them into the party. Jess saw India grasp Massimo's hand tightly—it was the first time since her stabbing that she had been out in Hollywood society, and her naturally shy personality was showing.

Jess helped her out, introducing the couple to some friendly types she knew, then began to work the room. She disliked the networking part of her job, but knew it was necessary. She fended off some awkward requests for representation from some 'beyond help' cases but took numbers from those she would like to work with.

Two hours into the party, she escaped to the pool where only a few people were standing around. Thankfully, the night had a cool breeze, and Jess closed her eyes, breathing in the fresh air before she returned to the party.

"I take it you're accepting new clients now."

Jess turned at the sound of his voice. Teddy Hood sat in a dark alcove, nursing his drink in his hand. He looked shattered. "Mr. Hood?"

"I called your office a year ago. I was desperate. I asked for your help to save my daughter from a miserable existence."

Jess frowned. He was drunk. "Mr. Hood..."

"Teddy." He sipped his drink again. Jess could feel the anger radiating from him. "Your office told me you weren't taking on new clients. So I went elsewhere to someone I shouldn't have trusted. I lost entire custody of my daughter, Ms. Olden, and today she tried to kill herself. My eight-year-old daughter took a bunch of my ex-wife's pills."

Jess was shocked to her core. "God... I am so sorry..."

"...and I keep thinking what would have happened if Jess Olden had said *yes* to me a year ago. Would DJ be living with me or at least half the time with me? Would she be happy?"

"Teddy, there's no way of knowing..."

He looked up at her, and his bright blue eyes were cold. "You're the best. Everyone says so. If you could have just said *yes* to one more client."

"Teddy..."

"No. It's too late now. Just do me one favor... when someone begs for help in the future, don't turn them away."

He got up, putting his glass down and pushing past her. She watched him stalk to the front of the house and disappear. Jess felt as if she had been punched in the stomach. His eight-year-old kid tried to kill herself? Jesus, how bad was it living with Dorcas Prettyman? Was her vile personality worse than even Jess knew?

She went to the bathroom and locked the door behind her, letting a few tears come. Teddy Hood's attack was completely unwarranted, she knew, but it had hit home. *I was caring for India*, she thought, *I was making sure the man who tried to have her killed was put away for the rest of his life. This is not my fault.*

Jess pulled herself together and went back to the party,

but the spark had gone out for her. Eventually she told the others she had a headache and to enjoy the rest of the party, but she was heading home.

When she got back to her condo, she changed into her sweats and tied her long dark hair up in a bun before checking online for any news about Teddy Hood's daughter. The entertainment reporters were only now picking up the story, and as expected, Dorcas was milking it. Jess's eyes narrowed as she watched the movie star make her entrance to the hospital, scarves and fur coat (real, ugh) as she wailed about her 'darling daughter.'

Right... Jess wondered just how bad it had gotten for the young kid. Eight. God. She looked up photographs of the girl—Dinah-Jane, DJ—and saw how happy she looked with her father and how cowed she was with her mother. In the most recent pictures, the girl's eyes looked way too old for her years, and there were dark circles under them. In paparazzi shots that were obviously set up by her mother, DJ was holding her mother's hand, or rather it looked like she was being dragged, her arm held at an awkward angle to accommodate her mother's pace rather than DJ's.

Jess gritted her teeth. She, too, had grown up with a narcissist father from whom she had been estranged for many years, happily so, as his toxic, aggressive, and fragile masculinity had been so utterly destructive she could only imagine what an eight-year-old would go through dealing with it.

She chewed her lip. Did she really want to get involved with this case after the horrors of her last big one? Yes. The thought came to her unbidden, but she shook her head. "Wait up, girl. This isn't your fault, so why do you feel so guilty?"

But she did, and she couldn't shake that feeling for the next few days. She enjoyed Christmas with her family—her non-DNA-sharing family, that is—but she kept checking the news for any update on DJ Hood's health. The girl was out of danger, thankfully, but still sick. There was talk of kidney damage. "Please, God, no." Jess whispered. Why the hell was she so invested in this?

Because you know, Jessica Olden, that had you taken this case, you would have won. You know Dorcas Prettyman of old; you know how she operates.

"Fuck it." Jess checked the clock. It was after midnight, but she made some calls and found out the information she needed. Pulling her jeans on, she grabbed her keys and went out to the car. Driving in LA at night was always kind of cool with the quieter streets and the lights, but tonight, Jess had only one focus.

She parked the car outside of the small apartment building and ran to the door, buzzing the intercom until a gruff voice answered. "It's me. Jess Olden."

The voice was silent, then she heard the door click, and she pulled it open and ran up the stairs.

He was waiting at the door, his expression unfriendly

and confused. "What do you want?" Teddy Hood was still as angry as she had seen him earlier as Jess reached him, breathless. She didn't try to exchange pleasantries, just fixed him with a steady look.

"I want to help you, Teddy. I'm going to get your daughter back for you."

CHAPTER FIVE – MY BLOOD

L*os Angeles*

TEDDY HOOD HAD SLAMMED the door in her face the first five times, but Jess kept going back. He buzzed her into the building every time, and Jess wondered if he just wanted to humiliate her as a punishment.

The sixth time, on New Year's Eve, she hadn't actually expected him to be let in, thinking he might be in a bar somewhere, drowning his sorrows. The news on DJ was that she had been released from hospital, her kidney damage a lot less serious than first feared, and was now 'at home, resting with her loving mother.'

Jess had smirked at that, but there was no humor in it. Where the hell were the people protecting this kid? Where were Children and Family Services? What about her school? Someone, somewhere should have raised alarm bells about letting her go home with her mother, right? But no, and it made Jess mad. So, she kept going back to Teddy Hood's apartment.

He buzzed her in as normal, then as she climbed the stairs, expecting him to slam the door, she was surprised to see him standing in the doorway, staring at her. He looked disheveled, maybe as if he'd just woken from a nap, his dark beard getting too long, his blue eyes red... and it kind of worked on him. Jess ignored the faint curl of desire in her stomach and nodded at him. "Teddy."

She waited for the door to slam, but instead, Eddy turned and disappeared back into the apartment, leaving the door open for her. Jess had a moment of pause—she was about to step into a strange man's apartment alone—an angry strange man at that.

But she never backed down. She walked in, expecting a cliché mess of an apartment, empty pizza boxes, half-drunk bottles of scotch. Instead she found a warmly lit living room lined with bookshelves, a beautifully carved wood coffee table with an empty coffee mug and an open paperback book. A huge dog, all fluff, was laying on a rug in front of the television, and he or she got up now and lumbered over to Jess, sniffing her hand, then rolling over for a belly rub.

Jess bent and fussed the dog. "She's beautiful. What breed is she?"

"Mixed. German Shepherd and St. Bernard."

"She's gorgeous."

Teddy's eyes weren't any friendlier. "Do you want a drink?"

"Tea or coffee would be good."

He gave a stiff nod and jerked his head at the couch, "Sit down."

He disappeared into what she assumed was a kitchen. She looked around. The apartment was nothing like she would expect of a movie star: small, compact, efficient, but what personal touches there were, she liked. A scented candle guttered on the window sill, a fresh clean fragrance like clean linen or the open air. The dog was settled back down again and gave a heavy sigh. It made Jess feel sleepy and she relaxed a little.

Teddy came back and handed her a mug of tea. "It's chamomile."

"Things are getting wild." She said with a mischievous smile and was gratified by the amused twitch of his mouth.

"No parties tonight? On New Year's?" He sat down next to her, setting his own steaming mug of tea on the table.

"Nope. I had something better to do."

Teddy leaned back and studied her. "I'm sorry for what I said at the party. It wasn't your fault."

"It's okay. I get it. How's DJ?"

"As far as I've been told, she's doing well. I wanted to..." He sighed and rubbed his face. "I don't get a say in anything anymore. I think she should be seeing a psychologist at the very least or have some time away from Dorcas's little world of Herself. DJ... DJ is a tomboy; she loves books, running, climbing, hiking, dogs…" He looked over at his own pet and smiled. "She would love Niko."

"She hasn't met her?"

Teddy shook his head. "I've been denied access for a year except for birthdays and video chatting. A *year*."

"How?" She knew the basics of the case having researched it, but she wanted to hear it from him.

"Dorcas is a very rich woman. Family money as well as her career earnings."

Jess nodded. "From what I hear, that money is fast drying up. She hasn't had a good role in a couple of years. Hollywood took your side."

"Fat lot of good it does me." Teddy stopped, sighed, and ran his hand through his dark hair. "Sorry. I don't mean to sound self-pitying… it's my kid, you know?"

"I know. Look, for what it's worth, I'm sorry I didn't take your case last year. My focus was on putting the man who tried to kill India away for life."

Teddy nodded. "I realize that, and I understand. But right now, I don't see how you're going to get DJ back for me. Dorcas has every judge in LA on her side."

"Nope. Not all of them can be bought."

"But they are randomly assigned, so I don't see…"

"Teddy, I did my research. You've only been in front of two judges so far, both who went to Dorcas's alma mater. Now whether that was coincidence, I don't know, but I do know those two judges have never ruled differently on anything. *Anything.* If Dorcas got to one, she got to the other, and if you think case assignments can't be manipulated... First thing we're going to do is ask for a review of the case by another judge."

Teddy studied her. "Aren't you going to ask me if I am an abusive parent?"

"Teddy... I have history with Dorcas. I know what kind of woman she is."

"She lies."

"Yes."

There was a small grin starting on his mouth. "How do you know I don't lie?"

Jess fixed him with a steady look. "I don't, yet. But you know who I do believe, without question?"

"Your own experience?" Teddy was openly grinning now, and she had to chuckle, but she shook her head.

"No," she said gently, "I believe DJ."

That got him, she could tell. He nodded and got up, turning his face away from her, and Jess saw the gentle shake of his shoulders. She let him have a moment, then got up and went to him, placing her hand on his shoulder. "Teddy. I will do everything in my power to get DJ back for you. Everything."

He met her gaze and something unspoken passed between them. Jess felt it deep in her belly, a curl of desire, but also of kinsmanship.

"Thank you. I mean it. Thank you for coming back. Thank you for not giving up on me."

THE MAN DORCAS had hired to follow Teddy called her even though it was late. She would want to know this. "It's me."

Dorcas Prettyman sounded three sheets already. "What is it?"

"That girl I've seen coming here? Tonight, she went in... and hasn't come out yet."

There was a silence on the other end of the phone. "You have a photograph?"

"I'll send it through now."

DORCAS FELT a thrill of adrenaline go through when she saw the photograph. Jessica Olden. *Well... fuck.* The one lawyer she knew for sure couldn't be bought. So, Teddy had hired her... or was fucking her

Or both. Dorcas hissed out a breath between her teeth. Whatever he was doing with her, it wasn't good news for Dorcas. She'd sailed by in the custody and settlement battles by calling in favors and by blowing more ancient, but powerful white men in both the judiciary system and in the media than she could count, but this was something new. She had heard that Olden had turned Teddy down a year before, so what had changed now?

She called her guy back. "Can you get someone to tail the lawyer, too?"

"She's a lawyer?"

"Yes. A powerful one. So, I want any dirt on her. I

mean, *anything*. Go through her trash if you have to. I want every inch of her life scrutinized."

"You got it, boss."

Dorcas ended the call and went upstairs. She hovered outside DJ's closed door but decided against checking on her daughter. Since coming home from the hospital, DJ had kept herself to herself. She'd ignored the reporters clamoring outside the mansion when she got home and went inside. That was okay with Dorcas—her daughter didn't steal focus when Dorcas played her part of the suffering, martyred mother.

They were spinning it that DJ found the pills at Teddy's place—or rather Dorcas insinuated it. They couldn't come right out and say it because everyone knew Teddy had no access to his daughter. So, when a reporter came right out and asked her if she was accusing Teddy of giving DJ the pills, Dorcas emphatically denied it. "We just don't know where she could have gotten them from… or how long she had kept them hidden."

Dorcas smirked to herself remembering it. The inconvenience of DJ's suicide attempt was far outweighed by the ground she had gained with the attention to herself. The loving mother role. It certainly outstripped the *pap* strolls she had forced DJ to go on, where her daughter could not be entreated to smile once.

Far outstripped. Hmm. Maybe she should up the concerned mother routine some more. She'd already reached her own bedroom but turned back and went to DJ's room. She opened the door a crack, but then heard her daughter's quiet sobs and decided against going in to her. She hated the whole tears thing. Dorcas closed the door and went to bed.

Tomorrow she would have to regroup. Figure out what she had to do about Teddy and Jess Olden, and what to do about her daughter. For the first time in DJ's short life, Dorcas was beginning to see the usefulness of her child's existence.

She still took a valium before she went to sleep.

CHAPTER SIX – SEVEN DEVILS

ew York

"Knock, knock." Jess grinned at her friend as she poked her head around the door to the physical therapy suite. India, sweaty and breathless, smiled at her, but Jess could see the strain in her face. "I don't mean to interrupt."

Clare, the physio helping India, smiled back at her. "We just finished up. I think you saved my life... someone's grumpy today."

"Not *that* grumpy."

"You've threatened to slash my tires three times already."

India grumbled to herself as Clare and Jess laughed, then the physio left them alone. India moved with obvious pain even after all these months. Jess looked at her sympathetically as India downed an entire bottle of water. "Is the pain still bad, boo?"

India nodded. "Clare and the docs keep telling me it'll take time for the nerves to heal, and that by strengthening my core, it'll happen faster. But, God, some days…"

"Somedays it just feels like an uphill battle?"

India nodded, then smiled sheepishly at her friend. "Sorry. Wallowing in self-pity today. I have no right. I'm here, I'm alive." She chewed her lip. "Sun's injuries were much worse than mine, and yet here he is on tour already, doing dance routines I couldn't do… even if I *could* dance." She grinned then. "Sorry, Jessie. How are you doing?"

"Good." Jess helped her friend up, seeing her wobble a little. India's injuries had been serious, but she had seemed to recover quickly. Jess now realized she had been hiding how much pain she had been in. "I took Teddy Hood's case."

"Oh, I am glad. That poor man."

Jess smiled. Trust India to know the truth of the matter. "I take it you've met Dorcas Prettyman?"

India shuddered. "A few times at benefits. The woman is faker than Milli Vanilli."

"Okay, Grandma, get up-to-date with the put downs." Jess grinned as India laughed.

"Sorry. Fuzzy-brained. But yeah, she's a pill, to put it mildly. And," India pulled on her sweater, "someone who really, really should *not* be allowed near vulnerable kids. Trying to kill yourself at eight. God."

"Right? Anyway, it took some persuading, but Teddy's agreed to me helping him."

"You might have to play dirty, because Dorcas will."

"I know. And screw her... all that matters is DJ." Jess watched India struggled into her jeans, and for the first time noticed the swell of her belly. "Boo... is that what I think it is?"

India looked away from her friend. "If you're asking if I'm pregnant, then no. But I'm having some treatment which makes me a little bloated. That and the scars... I feel so sexy right now." She tried to make a joke of it, but Jess could see something was upsetting her.

"What is it?"

India hesitated, then shook her head. "Nothing. Really, I'm just having a low mood day. Ignore and distract."

Jess hugged her. "You're allowed to get angry, you know. Lazlo was saying the other day he is surprised you haven't had a freak-out yet. Not even when your fa—when LeFevre was put away. You took it so calmly."

"What good is getting angry going to do? I can't change any of it. I'm just grateful Sun and I both made it, and no one else got hurt. Listen, I'm starving. Have you time to go grab lunch?"

"Always for you, boo."

OVER SANDWICHES AT KATZ'S, Jess probed her friend a little more, and India, albeit reluctantly, admitted she hadn't been sleeping. "I feel... guilty."

"For what?"

"All this crap... everything, everyone's lives so disrupted because of me. People putting off things to serve my purposes. You, Lazlo... Massimo's talking about retiring for good. He's only forty, Jess, and at the point of breaking Hollywood. There's Oscar buzz for his last film, but he doesn't seem at all interested."

Jess nodded sympathetically. "Darling, Massimo is a grown man and he loves you. I know he found his true passion when he met you."

"But I'm not a career, I'm his lover. What is he going to do staying home with me or coming on tour when I do get back to work?"

"You feeling crowded?"

India shook her head. "No, it's not that. I would spend every minute of every hour with him, but that isn't the real world. He worked hard for what he has, for everything."

"So did you, boo, and one day, two psychopaths decided to take that away from you. You haven't been the center of all our attention for nothing, Indy. You nearly died. That would have destroyed us all. One day, it might be me or Laz or Coco or Massi in that position, and you would do the same for us as we have for you. There's no guilt here. Just family."

JESS DROVE India back to her apartment, noticing her friend seemed a little brighter after their lunch. She would talk to Lazlo, however, because she was troubled by India's confession. It seemed to Jess that her friend was slipping into a depression—not surprising after the hell she had been through.

And Jess wondered if killing Braydon Carter had changed something in India, if something in her had been lost when she had been forced to do that. India claimed she didn't regret it one bit, but Jess knew her friend. Taking another human life, even if it was in self-defense and to avenge Sun's shooting and her mother's murder, wasn't something that would sit well with India.

Massimo had talked privately with Lazlo about it, but no one had breached the subject with India. Jess sighed. So much damage everywhere.

She got back to her office to find her assistant on the phone and waving her down. "It's Judge DeMaio from LA."

Jess went into the office and picked up the phone. "Lindy, hi. Thank you for calling me back."

"Like I said in my email, Jess, I can't guarantee anything, but from what you have told me, we can move to at least grant limited access in the wake of the appeal."

Jess nodded. "Thank you… and off the record?"

Lindy DeMaio, seventeen years a family court judge, laughed humorlessly. "This case disgusts me, Jess. Let's take Dorcas Prettyman down."

LOS ANGELES

. . .

TEDDY READ through his lines one more time, then put the script down. He'd read them at least fifteen times in the last hour, and yet still he had no idea what they were. He couldn't get Jess Olden out of his mind, and it was bugging him.

He believed her when she told him she would get DJ back for him; he could see the passion in her eyes for her work. It gave him hope.

But it also gave him anxiety. He didn't want her to be wrong. He didn't want to be disappointed in *her*. It made him feel that if it happened, that he would lose faith in *all* people.

For DJ. DJ who called him when she was permitted to, who cried down the phone, breaking his heart, asking him why he couldn't see her. He wanted to scream that it was because Mommy was a liar, Mommy was cruel, but he could not do it to his daughter. DJ knew her mother; she didn't need it confirmed. But every day Teddy dreaded the call. The call that told him that this time, DJ had been successful. That DJ was dead.

He tried to push the thought away now, but he tasted bile and had to get to the bathroom in his trailer to throw up.

He heard someone banging on the door. "Ted? Teddy? We're ready in five."

The director. "Sure thing, buddy, be right there."

Teddy rinsed his mouth out in the sink, then decided to brush his teeth. His costar in the next scene wouldn't want his vomit breath all over her. As he brushed, his eye was caught by the five little plastic beakers lined up on the shelf. Later, after filming was over for the day, his assistant would watch him pee into one and then take it to the drug testing unit assigned by the court.

More of Dorcas's machinations. Teddy, unlike most Hollywood stars, had never been one for drugs except for a joint, once a week after work years ago. Still, Dorcas had managed to insist on mandatory drug testing before she would allow DJ to even call her father. Fuck it, he had nothing to hide. His tests were always clean, and Dorcas was beginning to lose ground on her claims, especially now.

Which gave him hope that Jess Olden could do something to help him, to help DJ. *I believe DJ.* When she had said those words, something had changed in him, in his feelings of hopelessness. In his feelings for Jess. Because it wasn't just that she promised to fight for custody for him.

It was *her*...

He didn't want to admit he was attracted to her, because, God damn it, he was fighting for his child. Why was sex on his mind? Now?

But over the past few weeks, they had spent a lot of time together: at his apartment, at her office in New York, and Jess had been nothing but professional.

But she made him laugh, and that was something he hadn't felt for months, maybe even years. Better still, he didn't feel guilty about it. Jess's humor bordered on the sarcastic, and she made fun of his superstar actor status in such a way that he couldn't be offended, even if he'd been more sensitive. Jess knew the industry he was in and her irreverence for it matched his own. God, it was nice to meet someone like that.

And, Christ, she was beautiful: that thick, dark hair with the red highlights; the almond-shaped eyes and clear skin; the smile that was part goofy, part devastatingly sexy; the body honed by yoga; the long, shapely legs.

Teddy let out a long breath. *Calm down.* Getting a hard-on right now wasn't an option. The thought amused him as he headed out to shoot his scene.

DORCAS SWEPT into her kitchen the next morning, glancing at her daughter sitting quietly at the breakfast table. Dorcas nodded at her, but DJ looked away.

Dorcas turned her attention to Johanna, their cook. "I'll make DJ's breakfast," she told her, to Johanna's shock. "I think this is the perfect time to bond with my daughter. We'll see you later."

Johanna and DJ shared a confused look, but the older woman nodded and left the room. For a moment, Dorcas stood, trying to remember what eight-year-old kids ate for breakfast. She heard DJ's small sigh. "Cereal, Mom. Bottom shelf in the pantry. The pantry is in front of you."

Dorcas let that jibe go, giving a tinkling laugh. "I know, darling." She grabbed the box and looked for a bowl. DJ got up and went to get one, gently taking the cereal box from her mother.

"I'll do it."

Dorcas gave up, watching what her daughter did. Only a tiny voice in the back of her mind asked how far from reality had she really come that she didn't know how to serve her own daughter breakfast?

Had she *ever* served her daughter breakfast?

Dorcas pushed the thought aside and made herself some coffee. "I'll do better tomorrow, now that I know where everything is."

DJ was chewing her cereal slowly, and her eyes, too old for her age, looked at her mother cautiously. "Why?"

Dorcas swallowed back a retort and smiled. "Because we don't spend enough time together, darling, and that's my fault. I've been so busy helping out other people's children I neglected you. Let's make friends, okay? What can I do to make you happy, sweetie?"

DJ finished her mouthful and fixed Dorcas with a steady gaze. "Let me see Daddy."

Dorcas sighed. "Dinah…"

"DJ."

"DJ, you know that's not possible."

She watched her daughter's face crease in pain, and somewhere deep inside her, something pulled at her heart.

"I just want to see my daddy." DJ said, putting down her spoon.

"Have you finished eating?"

DJ nodded.

"Then get down and go get ready for school."

"Can Johanna take me?"

Dorcas gave up. "Fine."

DJ disappeared back to her own bathroom, and Dorcas drained her coffee, picking pieces of cereal out of the remnants of DJ's breakfast and crunching them between her teeth. Maybe she should let DJ see Teddy… at least she would appear magnanimous. The press was already starting to turn on her after DJ's suicide attempt—someone at the hospital had talked about Dorcas' diva-like behavior there.

And it would maybe distract Jess Olden from going after her in the way Dorcas knew she would. She'd never liked the other woman—she was way too sharp, sarcastic, and quick for Dorcas's intellect—or lack thereof. Plus, the woman had a natural beauty that Dorcas couldn't have even without her multiple surgeries.

Yeah, undercutting Jess Olden was a pretty good motive for Dorcas to let Teddy see DJ, and if it kept her daughter partially on her side…

…plus, it gave Dorcas someone to blame when DJ fell ill. She quickly pushed that idea away. No, she would not go there.

Not unless she was forced to.

CHAPTER SEVEN – I WANNA BE YOURS

New York

MASSIMO VERDI LOOKED at his fiancée as they walked around the empty apartment. Outside the wall-to-ceiling windows, the view over Central Park was incredible, but India didn't seem to be enthused about it. Massimo asked the realtor to give them a moment alone, and he waited until she had stepped out to wrap his arms around his lover.

"What is it, baby?"

She leaned into him. "I'm sorry, I'm just in a funk today, and I don't know why. And the apartment is great."

"But?"

"But... it feels just like Laz's apartment. It's even got the same view albeit a different angle of the park. And Manhattan… would you hate me if I said I was kind of over it?"

Massimo pressed his lips to her temple. "Of course not, Indy. And it is a nice apartment, and a good investment, but we don't have to live here. We can live anywhere you want."

"*We* want. That's what's important, and if you like this place…"

"Like I said, I'd look at it as an investment and somewhere we can stay when we are in the city. Or the twins can stay here," he said, talking about his younger siblings, Gracia and Francesco, who were at film school in Rome. "You know they'll want to spend the summer in New York. But as for us, for our home… the world is our playground now, baby."

India turned and kissed him softly. "I honestly would live anywhere with you, Massi. But… I want a home. Somewhere we can have dogs, where our kids, if we have any, can play outside. Somewhere… private."

Massimo tightened his arms around her. "So, we'll look elsewhere. Anywhere in particular?"

She smiled. "Somewhere near water."

"Deal. Look, let's leave this for now and go grab some lunch. Then I want to take you home and do rude things to you." He grinned and winked at her, and she laughed. He could see her body relax.

"You have a deal."

. . .

THROUGH LUNCH, India's mood improved, and she became more like his old Indy again: funny, silly, goofy. They walked back to Lazlo's apartment, fingers interlaced, and when they were inside alone, Massimo stripped her slowly even before they reached the bedroom.

India giggled as he swept her into his arms and onto the bed. "No fair, you still have all your clothes on."

"That's right, *Bella*, and for now, that's going to be the way it stays. I'm in charge now."

India's eye lit up at his masterful tone. "Oh, really?"

Massimo grinned and covered her body with his. "Oh, yes... just lay back and let your man take care of you." His lips met hers, then drifted down her body, stopping to suck at her nipples. His tongue trailed down her belly, around her navel, and then his mouth found her sex. He heard her contented sigh as her body relaxed. Massimo flicked his tongue around her clit, feeling it respond, harden, and quiver, then he plunged deep into her cunt, tasting her sweet honey, making her cry out, her sex swelling and taking on the most glorious pink flush.

"I want you inside me," India panted, her fingers tangling in his hair, and Massimo relented, freeing his already diamond-hard cock from his pants and thrusting into her. He never took his eyes off of hers as they made love, and India stroked his face as they moved together.

"I love you so much, Massi."

Massimo responded by kissing her so fiercely that he tasted blood, and she giggled, breathlessly. "Tiger."

He laughed. "Only for you."

They came together, shuddering and sighing their love for the other, and then lay talking until twilight fell outside the windows. India napped while Massimo dressed, and he watched her sleep, her lovely face relaxed now.

Lately he had been wondering about her emotional health. Since the stabbing, since killing Carter, she had gone through so much with the physical recovery. She had begged off seeing a psychologist, telling her loved ones she didn't want everything in her life to revolve around what had happened. India was frustrated, certainly—she'd tried to work, to write some new songs, but there was a block she couldn't get past. Even seeing Sun and Tae—Sun now recovered and healthy after his own shooting—hadn't pulled her entirely out of it.

MASSIMO SHRUGGED into his sweater now and went into the living room. He checked his messages, ignoring most of them, then called his agent. "Hey, how's things, Massi?"

His agent, Gen, was his representative here in the US, and Massi had enjoyed getting to know her. Gen was a sweetheart to talk to, but a hard-ass when it came to getting him the best scripts and good money—he was, after all, still trying to conquer the American market after years of being Italy's number one heartthrob. For a few months, Massimo had eschewed work to look after India, but lately she had been encouraging him to get back out there and see what was available.

Gen sounded excited now. "I just got a call from Bymax

Studios. They're casting a thriller I think you would be perfect for. Teddy Hood is already attached, and the writers are Leman and Holly Jones."

Massimo whistled. The Jones' were the hottest writers in Hollywood right now, and whenever they were attached to a movie, everyone wanted in. "And the studio called *me*?"

Gen laughed. "Don't sound so amazed. Apparently, the Jones' wrote the part with you in mind. You'll play the antagonist to Teddy's protagonist, and Tiger Rose will play the woman caught in the middle between both of you."

"Sounds interesting," Massimo chuckled, "although I'm not sure it's a compliment to have a villainous role written specifically for me."

"Nah, it's all good. The villain's the part that'll get the Oscar."

"Ha, now you are dreaming. But, sure, send the script over."

"Already in your email. Listen, I know you've been out of the loop with India recovering, but this could be the very film that pushes you over the edge. It would mean spending some time in LA."

"Shouldn't be a problem, but I will have to discuss it with India."

"Of course."

Massimo thanked his agent and ended the call. The idea of the new film intrigued him. And it was a weird coincidence that Teddy Hood was slated to costar—especially now that Jess was working with him. He put in a call to her now. "Hey, kiddo."

"Hey, loser."

Massimo and Jess had very quickly fallen into their best friend roles when they had met, forever busting each other's chops, and teaming up to tease India. They shared the same irreverent sense of humor and fierce loyalty to those they loved,

"Guess what? I may be doing a film with your new client."

"Teddy?"

"The very one."

Jess chuckled. "So, you want some dirt?"

"Just an impression. Will I like him?"

Jess laughed again. "I'm sure he'll think you're a very pretty girl, Massi."

"Very funny. No, really, what's your impression?"

There was a short silence on the other end of the phone. "He's... nice."

Massimo snorted. "What a wonderful lukewarm way to describe someone."

Jess chuckled. "Sorry. I was trying to be, well, unbiased, Truth is, Mass, I like him very much. He's been through hell with this divorce, and yet he still keeps on going. That's impressive to me. Although I will judge him forever for marrying the evil bitch."

"Ah, yes, Dorcas Prettyman."

"Have you met her?"

"Unfortunately, once. She and my ex Valentina got into it on the panel of the Venice Film Festival a couple of years ago. Delightful woman, and by delightful, I mean a Gorgon."

Jess snorted. "Oh, coffee just shot out of my nose, but it was totally worth it. Yup, that's Dorcas, alright." She sighed. "She's playing games at the moment, and I'm still trying to... well, never mind that. You asked about Teddy? You'd like him, Massi."

Massimo grinned to himself, noticing how her voice softened when. "*You* like him."

"Of course, he's my client."

"I wasn't asking. You like *like* him, Jessie."

"What are you, twelve?" Jess's voice was full of mock-outrage, but she laughed with him. "I admit... he's easy to like."

"Go for it, Jessie."

"Ha." Jessica gave a short cough of self-consciousness—which was when Massimo knew for sure she had a crush on Teddy Hood. Jess wasn't one to feel embarrassed about a potential fling. Maybe Teddy meant more than that?

Massimo looked up as India appeared, hair mussed up, rubbing her eyes and looking for all the world like the twelve-year-old kid Jess had just accused *him* of being. Massimo grinned at her. "India's up. You want to talk to her?"

"Yes, please."

He handed the phone to his fiancée. "Jessie's got a new boy crush."

He heard Jessica protest loudly as he and India laughed. He heard Indy begin to grill her friend about Teddy Hood as he grabbed his laptop and checked his emails. Sure enough, the script for *Blackwater Heart* was there.

With one ear listening to India's obviously fun conversation with her friend, Massimo sat down and began to read.

JESS GOT the call late on the Friday afternoon, and she immediately drove to Teddy's apartment. "Dorcas has decided to allow you visitation again."

Teddy's eyes grew big. "That was fast work."

"Nothing to do with me... which is why this gives me pause." Jess didn't smile, and he stood aside to let her in, the excitement in his eyes fading. He followed Jess into his living room, offering her tea which she thanked him for. As she waited, Niko came over to her and stuck her muzzle in Jess's hand. Jess fussed the dog, kissing her silky head. She didn't see Teddy watching her.

As he sat down with the full mugs, he nodded for her to go on. "Teddy, from what you've told me, from what I know of Dorcas personally, this is totally out of character. Now, let's not get carried away; she's saying she'll allow supervised visits during the week as before, then a whole weekend, once a month."

"That's better than before... so why aren't I celebrating?"

Jess sipped her tea before continuing. "On the ride over, I was figuring out the reasons for this about face. One... it's what DJ wants, and the suicide attempt was a wake-up call. Dorcas has finally put her child first."

Teddy snorted. "As if."

"Well, quite. Hear me out. Two... she knows the press is beginning to turn on her, just like Hollywood has done. Damage control."

"That *is* probably the reason," Teddy acknowledged, "but to be honest, that really doesn't bother me as long as I get to see DJ."

"Yeah, okay, that's fair, but I still urge caution."

"Because?"

Jess smiled grimly. "Because of reason three. She's setting you up for something."

Teddy stared at her. "Like what?"

"That's what I *don't* know. And, listen, I hope I'm wrong. I really do."

Teddy got up, pacing the way he had when she had first come here. He was wearing the navy sweater she liked, that looked so good on him again. The dark beard was thicker if not longer, and his hair stuck up as if he had been laying down. Damn, he was cute... Jess saw a script on the coffee table and wondered if it was the same film that Massimo had told her about.

"Look, Jessie, whatever her reason, I get to see DJ. That's huge."

She smiled at his casual use of her nickname. It meant he trusted her and she liked that. "It is, Teddy, it is huge, and I'm delighted for you. Just... let's just keep our counsel."

"What do you suggest?" He sat down next to her instead of the easy chair opposite, and Jess felt a small rush of desire as she caught the scent of his cologne, woody and spicy. His muscled thighs in jeans were way too distracting, so close to hers.

Concentrate. You're a professional and this is about his child... "I say we act as if we're pleasantly surprised and go along with the custody agreement. Don't go over by even a minute. Spend the weekends doing the dad thing but play Dorcas at her own game. Don't call the *paps*, but go places where they'll automatically be, celebrity hotspots for families, that kind of thing. Obviously, do what is best for DJ, but the occasional visit to shop at the Grove or get some ice cream somewhere the other stars take their kids wouldn't hurt once in a while. Just so Dorcas doesn't win the PR battle she thinks she will."

Teddy grimaced but nodded. "DJ is more of a Sunlight Books kind of kid."

"God, I was, too."

"Last week when you were twelve."

Jess grinned. "Ha ha. I'm thirty-five, thank you. Obviously at your great age..."

"Five years older than you, Olden. And your age is in your name."

Jess stuck out her tongue at him, and he grinned. "Anyway, yes, so once in a while. Just so you're out there, being the good father that you are." She saw the smile on his face fade. "What?"

He hesitated. "What if I've been kidding myself, Jessie? What if I'm *not* a good father?"

Jess hated the look in his eyes now, and she put her hand on his. "You are. Believe me, I've seen my share of bad fathers, from the narcissistic to the downright psychopathic. You wouldn't be in this much pain if you didn't love DJ with your whole heart. We may not have known each other long, but I know on instinct that you are a great father. Not a perfect one because they don't exist. But DJ loves you."

Teddy looked down at her hand on his and slowly, and very deliberately turned his hand over and linked his fingers with Jess's. Her heart began to thump against her ribs too hard, and she gently extricated her hand, smiling to soften the rejection. "It's not that I don't... you're my client, Teddy. Until this thing is..." Just looking into his cornflower blue eyes made her lose her thread, and Teddy smiled at her.

"For the next few moments, you're fired," he said softly and then his lips were against hers. God, that kiss... Jess felt it everywhere, in every cell in her body, and when he slid his hand into her hair, she was lost. "Jessie?"

"Yes?" God, she felt like a giddy teenager... which she hadn't felt like even when she *was* a teenager.

"Will you stay?"

Oh God, she wanted to. She *desperately* wanted to, but...

"I can't. I don't want to risk anything going wrong in our fight for DJ. Anything." She gently placed her palm against his cheek, her thumb stroking across the soft skin under his eye. "Believe me, this... *us*... I can't stop thinking about you, Teddy Hood. I haven't since I met you. But I promised you something and... if anyone found out, not only would my reputation would be sullied, but Dorcas would use it against you in a heartbeat."

Teddy leaned his forehead against hers and closed his eyes. "I know you're right, Jessie... it's just..."

"I know."

JESS SAID goodbye to him shortly after and drove back to her office, trying not to think of the feel of his soft lips against hers. Christ, it had taken all of her willpower not to jump his bones right then and there, but she was proud of herself. Proud... and not a little regretful. Her body was aching with longing, as it had been over the past few weeks as she got to know this kind, very un-movie-star-like man. Teddy Hood wasn't like any entertainer she had ever met. He was quiet, shy, and introspective, but he had a wicked sense of humor that matched hers, and she liked the way he lived, too. Nothing ostentatious, just his books, Niko, and she had noticed, a sizable vinyl collection. She had studied it once while he was making coffee, gratified that he had all of India's records and an eclectic ear.

Jess had started to live for the times they were together, even though she behaved professionally of course, but their natural chemistry meant that the meetings were always... *fun.* Apart from the seriousness of the situation with DJ, she found Teddy relaxed in her company even if he arrived at her office with a frown or opened the door to his apartment to let her in, and she could see the strain in his face.

And she wasn't imagining it. When he looked at her, his face lit up and his whole body language changed from defeat to... something else. *God,* she thought, *you sound like a high school girl with a crush.* But, she had to admit... she did have a crush on Teddy. That's all it is.

But Jess knew it was more than that. It wasn't just Teddy who lit up when they were together.

God damn it...

CHAPTER EIGHT – IT'S DEFINITELY YOU

Los Angeles

MASSIMO AND INDIA tried to travel to LAX incognito, but it was never going to happen. As they were jostled and harangued by paparazzi, India nudged Massimo. "Remember when we were sneaking around when we first met? Was it like this?"

Massimo grinned at her. "We had more of a reason to hide away back then, remember? Thank God we don't have to do that anymore for *that* reason. And I think if we had really tried, we could have flown in under the radar, but we chose to fly public air. We didn't exactly fly in Lazlo's private jet."

"I miss that thing."

"*You* were the one telling him to think of the environment." Massimo opened the door of the town car that was waiting for them and India got in.

"I still don't think he's entirely forgiven me for that," she said to him when he got in beside her.

Massimo stroke a strand of hair behind her ear. "He has. Are you okay? You're a little pale."

"Just a little nerve pain. They never show that in the movies, do they? People get shot and stabbed and walk it off in weeks. They don't show all the crappy after effects." India shrugged, and Massimo was happy to see, that despite her words, she seemed upbeat.

They were on the way to stay with Coco and Alex, and Massimo was due to meet with the producers of *Blackwater Heart* to discuss the role he was being offered. He had loved the script—Gen was right, it was a role that could garner acclaim if he nailed it.

And he was excited about a role for the first time in years. India, too, had read the script, and when she had finished, she tugged her spectacles from her face and told him straight. "Dude, if you don't do this, the wedding is off."

He had laughed but she looked serious. "This is... it's violent and tragic and beautiful, boo. Massi, God, as much as I love all your movies, this would beat them all."

"I know," he'd said, sitting down next to her. "But it would mean being in Los Angeles for at least three months."

"So? We can do that. I'll get to see Coco when she's

still preggo, and depending when filming starts, we might even be there when the baby is born. Call Gen," she urged him, making him laugh as she pushed him away when he tried to get fresh with her, "Call Gen and say yes and then you can come back and fuck me to celebrate."

MASSIMO REMINDED her of that now and she laughed. "And boy, you did. And guess what? We're gonna do it all over again later."

"In Coco's place? She'll be traumatized. She still hasn't forgotten when we were having phone sex that time."

India grinned. "Video sex. Man, that seems like a lifetime ago, doesn't it?"

"Sure does."

Massimo hooked his arm around her shoulders. "You know, if you wanted somewhere new…"

India grinned. "West coast, huh? I don't know, it's so hot here all the time."

He laughed. "For an Indian, you sure don't like the heat."

"Not full time, and as always," she wiggled her eyebrows at him, "context is everything."

COCO WAS DELIGHTED to see them, and India exclaimed that she was already showing.

"I know, I'm huge," Coco rolled her eyes and patted her

small bump. She laughed and hugged India and kissed Massimo's cheek. "Come on in."

Coco and Alex had a beautiful condo in Malibu, all whitewashed wood and space with views over the ocean. India exclaimed over the huge guest bedroom with its beachy vibe and clean lines. "Can I move in?"

Coco grinned. "Make yourself at home. And listen, before I forget, Alex and I talked, and if you do make this film, Massi, we want you both to stay here with us."

"Oh, we couldn't," India said, "we don't want to intrude."

Coco snickered. "On what? Alex and my sex life?"

"Ha ha."

"Now, enough talk. Come out to the deck. I've made a huge jug of sangria, and I can watch you two drink it and live through you vicariously. Alex had to shoot out for a meeting, but he's coming back as soon as he can. Then, Massimo, you and Alex can do the macho grilling thing like cavemen, and India and I can gossip and bitch about you, deal?"

India giggled as Massimo looked vaguely alarmed. Pregnancy had obviously made Coco hyperactive—and she wasn't low key to begin with.

In the end, India and Massimo showered and changed before Alex returned with Jess in tow. The lawyer grinned at her friends. "We must stop meeting like this."

"We mustn't," shot back India with a laugh, hugging her friend, "I like that we keep meeting on both coasts." She shot a conspiratorial glance at Coco who gave her a subtle nod. They had planned something, a little surprise for Jess, and now that she was here, they could put their plan into motion.

JESS TUGGED her coat off and went to splash water on her face. She had spent the morning in court with another client, hashing out a custody agreement for a singer and her ex-girlfriend. It had been fraught but finally resolved to everyone's satisfaction. Now, she could concentrate on Teddy's case.

In the week since they had kissed, she hadn't been able to get him out of her head, and it was bugging her, seriously bugging her. Jess didn't crush on people; she didn't have time for that crap. She either asked them out or forgot about them. But Teddy Hood was different. She kept thinking about those blue, blue eyes, that soft mouth on hers...

"Hey, Spacecakes. Wanna come help me out here?"

Jess looked up as she went back into the kitchen and saw Coco struggling with two huge pitchers of drink. Jess took them from her and carried them out onto the porch. It was March now and already warm, and Jess breathed in the ocean air. It always relaxed her, being near the water and she smiled as she saw India relaxing, too. When they had met in college, they both ditched classes now and again to go hang out on the beach and talk.

"Indy, how's the rehab going?"

India grimaced then laughed. "I just remember how much I hate working out."

"You don't seem to mind it with me," Massimo said with a grin and she laughed.

"Context is everything, my love." India glanced behind Jess. "Oh, hello. We have a visitor." She didn't sound that surprised though, and when Jess turned, she realized what the origin of the loaded glances between India and Coco had been about.

Teddy Hood stood behind her, looking as surprised—and happy—to see Jess as she was to see him. They stared at each other for a long moment, smiles spreading across their faces before Teddy shook himself, realizing that there were others in the room. "Hey, hi, everyone. I'm Teddy."

Massimo grinned, standing and shaking his hand. "We know, Teddy. It's good to meet you at last."

Jess swallowed hard, gathering herself as Teddy shook hands with everyone, and then, when he turned to her, he just grinned that crooked grin of his. "Hey, boss."

Jess gave a laugh, relieved that there was no awkwardness, and she hugged him. "Hey, loser."

"That's my pet name!" Massimo chuckled in mock anger, and Jess snickered.

"Yeah, well, who knew there were *two* of you?"

It broke the ice, teasing and being teased, and Jess was gratified that Teddy seemed at ease with her friends—her family—as the afternoon went on and slipped into dusk. India and Coco obviously had a plan, and that plan involved them carefully maneuvering around so that Jess and Teddy were always together.

But it felt so natural with him here as if he had always been a part of their little gang. He shared their same irreverent sense of humor, and, she thought now, he knew the same pain that they all had experienced. The cruelty of someone else, the panic and grief of nearly losing a loved one because of it. No wonder he fit in so well.

Jess didn't even recall when they had started to hold hands. Maybe after the third pitcher of cocktails that Coco had brought out, grinning to herself, secure in the knowledge she'd be the only sober one at the end of the night. Jess had sipped her drink with one hand, and as she rested her other on the arm of her chair, Teddy's hand had slid on top of hers, and their fingers had interlaced. It felt so nice, so... comforting... in her half-drunk state that she forgot her reservations and left her hand where it was. She met India's eyes and her friend smiled at her, obviously delighted. India nodded at Teddy and smiled. She mouthed something at Jess, but Jess couldn't make out what she had said.

Teddy and Massimo were discussing the film they were to make together, Alex asking them about the roles they were playing. Jess listened to them idly, but the drink had gotten to her, and she smiled lazily when Coco tapped her on the knee. "You'll stay tonight? We have plenty of guest rooms. Plenty," she said with meaning, cutting her eyes at Teddy meaningfully.

Jess rolled her eyes but couldn't help grinning. The

drink and the company had made her entire body relax, and when, one-by-one her friends turned in for the evening, leaving her and Teddy alone as night fell, she didn't raise any objection.

Teddy gazed at her and she met his eyes, the answer to his silent question in them. He leaned closer and their lips met, his tongue gently caressing hers as they kissed. Jess sank into the embrace, shedding all of her reservations. God, she wanted this man right here, right now; she didn't care about anything else.

"Am I still fired?" She murmured it against his lips, felt them curve up into a smile.

"For the next few hours, *yes*," he whispered back. Jess drew back and met his gaze, studying him.

Yes. Yes, this was going to happen.

She stood, offering him her hand, and he took it, rising, and they slowly walked hand-in-hand into the condo to one of the guest rooms.

Teddy stroked her cheek as they shut the door behind them. Jess leaned back against it as Teddy pressed his body against hers, and she could feel the hot length of his cock, already erect, against her belly.

"Jessica..." The way he said her name made her senses reel and as his lips found her throat, she closed her eyes and gave into the sweet sensations he was sending through her body.

She tangled her fingers in his hair as he unbuttoned her shirt, his lips on her breasts as he unclasped her bra, biting gently at her nipples before teasing the nubs with his tongue. Jess moaned and pulled at his sweater, jerking it roughly over his head in her need to feel his bare skin.

Teddy grinned as the motion made his hair stick up every which way, and Jess laughed at the sudden release of tension. She kissed him, pressing herself against him. "Take me to bed, Hood."

He lifted her into his arms and carried her to the bed, his eyes never leaving hers. "If you knew how long I've been fantasizing about this moment," he said, shaking his head and laughing.

"Ditto," Jess's fingers were at the fly of his jeans now, and she pushed them down, cupping her hand on his long, thick cock through his underwear, "since almost as soon as I met you."

"Ditto," he returned, and she laughed. He took her pants off, then she shimmied out of her underwear. Teddy sat back and sighed. "God, you're even more beautiful than I dreamed."

He pressed her back and pushed her thighs apart, and then his mouth was on her sex, licking, teasing, dipping deep inside her before flicking around her clit, making her shudder and groan with desire.

"God, Teddy..." Her fingers were pulling at his dark hair as electricity shot through every cell in her body. "I want to taste you, too."

They maneuvered around so she could free his cock from his underwear, and as she took him into her mouth, she could taste the salty, clean taste of his skin. She ran her tongue across the wide crest, the silky tip of his cock, and ran her fingers up and down the shaft as she sucked him.

"Jesus, Jess..."

She was almost at her peak when he withdrew from her mouth and gathered her to him. She helped him roll a condom down over his straining cock, and then with one powerful thrust, he was inside her. Jess's legs curved around his waist as their eyes met and held as they moved together. "Fuck me *hard*," she said, and he grinned, slamming his hips against hers until they were both coming, crying out the other's name, not caring if anyone else heard.

They fucked again on the floor, then in the ensuite shower, Teddy pressing Jess up against the cool tile and easing into her ass, biting down on her shoulder as they moved together slowly.

For Jess, who had always been uninhibited when it came to sex, it was a revelation to meet someone who could match her, kink for kink. Teddy didn't even blink when she asked him to take her roughly, didn't flinch when she clawed and fought with him as they fucked. It was so good to be held by him, but she enjoyed the tussles even more, the power struggle, the laughter that followed.

She fell asleep cradled in his arms, and when she woke, a few hours later, he was still holding her and it felt... right. She watched him sleep for a few moments, then not wanting to freak him out, she slid quietly from his arms and tugged on a robe hanging behind the bathroom door.

Teddy stirred, his arms seeking her, and as Jess watched him, a smile spread over his face and he murmured her name so tenderly that it made tears spring into her eyes.

That was the moment she knew she was in love with him.

CHAPTER NINE – STRESSED OUT

Los Angeles

DORCAS HAD BEEN RECEIVING information on Teddy and Jessica Olden for weeks now, but it soon bored her. If they were fucking, then they hid it well. After that evening when Jess had stayed longer than usual, Dorcas' detective had reported that they had either met in Olden's office or at Teddy's film set.

Boring, boring, boring. Dorcas had hoped to use her ex-husband's affair with his lawyer to cause trouble for him, but they weren't cooperating at all. Dorcas cheered herself up by wondering if Teddy was having problems getting it up. No that he'd ever had that problem with her. That was one of the things she missed most about him: Teddy Hood was the best lover she had ever had, bar none. His cock, so thick and long, could drive her into ecstasy, and she missed the way her cunt was sore and swollen for days after one of their marathon sex games.

Of course, she was a different person then. A freer person. Someone who didn't care about stardom and money and saving face. When she and Teddy had met, she had been drawn to his fun-loving ways, but also to the way he cared for her and for everyone around him. He'd just been beginning to get noticed, this cute boy from Washington State, his big blue eyes and dark hair making him the pin-up of every bored housewife and every college student she knew. Dorcas was already a star and could have had any man she wanted—but she wanted Teddy and he didn't stand a chance.

And, Christ, she had loved him, *really* loved him, and that had been a new thing for her. Teddy, yes, was easy to love, but she had thought they would be together for life. That his rising star would meet hers, and they would rule as Hollywood's power couple, the 'It' couple for decades.

Then Dinah-Jane was born, and Teddy's love seemed to transfer from Dorcas to his daughter. Was that fair? Hadn't the ardor between them cooled already before DJ was even conceived? Wasn't DJ the band-aid baby she'd agreed to have to keep him? Teddy had been so desperate to be a father…

She remembered the story his ex-girlfriend, another actress, had told in an interview about him after he and Dorcas had married. The ex had been complimentary about Teddy, no hard feelings, but had told the magazine that he had always wanted to be a father, and that she couldn't imagine Dorcas ever slowing her career for a child.

Dorcas had her revenge by planting stories that the ex-girlfriend was barren, that she had denied Teddy a child in the time they were together. Teddy was furious, his ex cut ties with him, and the damage was done. Dorcas remained unrepentant.

Dorcas flicked out the cigarette and buried the evidence in a plant pot. She kept the cigarettes hidden well away from the staff and from DJ, but once a week she gave into the craving. She figured it wasn't any worse than her other habits. She glanced down at her skinny arms now. If only you'd thought to insist on having me take blood tests, too, Teddy, she thought with a grim smile. She hadn't shot up in a while but still, she missed the heady rush of heroin through her veins.

Her dealer was getting annoyed with extending her line of credit, and she couldn't blame him. It wasn't as if she couldn't afford to clear her debt, it was just... why should she? She was Dorcas Prettyman, for fuck's sake!

Dorcas went inside now and padded up the stairs to her bed. DJ's bedroom door was open, and she could see her daughter reading quietly in bed. She went to the door. "Lights out now, DJ."

DJ pouted but put her book down. Dorcas felt a strange rush of... something and she went into the room, perching on the end of the bed. DJ had been much less distant from her since she had let her visit with Teddy again, something Dorcas knew she could use to her advantage when the time came.

She smoothed her daughter's head. "Goodnight, darling."

"Goodnight, Mommy." DJ closed her eyes and turned over, away from Dorcas. Dorcas stayed there for a beat, then got up and went to her own bedroom. The bed looked empty, too empty, and she wondered if she should booty-call one of her young admirers to come over. She needed to fuck, to be held.

Two birds with one stone. She called her dealer, a pretty young hustler called Rick and invited him over. "I have your money and then some. I'll pay you to spend the night."

"Have the cash ready and we'll talk." He broke the connection.

Slightly annoyed, Dorcas called down to the gate and told them to let Rick in when he arrived, then went to the bathroom to bathe. She'd make him pay for his obnoxiousness when his cock was buried deep inside her. She'd ride him until he begged her to stop.

Smirking, Dorcas slipped into the rose-scented water and awaited her date for the night.

JESS WAS GRINNING to herself as she rode the elevator up to her office. Less than an hour ago, she was laying in Teddy Hood's arms after a night of lovemaking, laughter, and talking. It had been two weeks since their first night together at Coco's house, and they hadn't spent a night apart since.

She was grateful for her friends giving her the push she needed to be with Teddy. The morning after that first time, no one had made fun or even raised an eyebrow, and she loved them for that. They'd enjoyed breakfast out on the deck with their friends, and Jess had perched on Teddy's knee as he fed her fruit.

They'd even shared a cab together back to her place where they'd made love again and then sat down to discuss his case as if they hadn't just been fucking all night. Jess was glad he could separate 'them' from work.

As she entered her office, however, her smile started to fade when she saw Bee, her assistant, waiting for her with a grim look on her face. "What's up?"

Bee ushered her into her office and shut the door. "We've got trouble. At least, I think it's trouble, it depends how seriously you take YouTuber drama."

Jess blinked. "What on earth...?"

Bee half-smiled. "Let me introduce you to the world of Spilling the Tea. Basically gossip, 'truth' seekers, and the ilk. Some genuine content creators, but also some real assholes."

"You've lost me entirely, but okay. So, what's the problem?"

Bee sat down. "One of the asshole-types is a vlogger called Taran Googe has decided that he's going to 'expose' "—and she used the air-quotes—"the truth behind Hollywood divorces. More specifically, the lawyers involved, and guess who his latest 'exposé' is about?"

Jess sighed. "Me."

"Yup."

"And what bullshit is he spouting?"

Bee looked uncomfortable. "He's starting on your involvement with the Prettyman and Hood divorce. You're lucky; he's doing a two-parter on you."

Jess shrugged. "So? Who pays attention to these things anyway?"

"Jess... he's released a teaser of the segment... and he talked to your father."

That was a cold, cold shot to the heart. "What? What the *fuck*?"

Bee nodded. "Now, we don't know if by 'talking' he means he called him and got to say hello before your father hung up, or he actually got an interview. What would be your thoughts on that?"

"I guess we'll see when the segment goes live." Jess sat back, looking out of the window. She hadn't talked to her father for nearly fifteen years; what could he possibly say about her that would be in any way relevant to the person she was now? They barely knew each other then, let alone now.

"You really don't want to shut it down?"

"I think it'll look worse if we make a fuss. This too shall pass and all that."

Bee looked unhappy. "Jess... I hate to say this, but YouTubers are influencers now. They make a fuss about something, it gets noticed. Look at Shane Dawson's documentaries."

"Who?"

Bee grinned. "Grandma."

Jess shrugged, smiling. "I honestly don't care, Bee. I haven't got anything to hide."

Bee chewed her lip. "Jess, what if they bring up the Houston thing?"

"With Simon? That's old news."

Bee got up. "Okay. Okay, but I'll let you know when this thing goes up on the net."

"Please. Then we can watch it together—get the popcorn ready." Jess twisted in her chair and flicked on her laptop, smiling her thanks at Bee. When she was alone, she checked her emails and then sat back, thinking about last night with Teddy.

HE HAD BEEN UPBEAT, talking about his day with DJ. The two of them had gone out to Venice Beach and spent the day eating way too much sugar and playing around.

"She's just... she's such a good kid, you know? Sometimes I worry that she's growing up too fast, but she seems okay."

Jess smiled at him. "I'm glad. I'd love to meet her at some point, but I understand that might be difficult."

Teddy shook his head. "I don't think it would be. You're my girlfriend; it would be weird for her not to meet you. Plus," he added with a roll of his eyes, "it would do her good to see both her parents with other people. She needs to get used to it."

Jess smiled but said nothing. Girlfriend. Something about that word had always made her want to run and hide, it sounded so teenager-ish. But... Teddy saying it sounded different. She wanted to be his girlfriend—more than a lover, a friend as well—and it made her happier than she liked to admit to hear him say it. She pulled herself up. Grow up, woman.

But Teddy made her senses reel every time she was near him, and it was a new sensation for her. When he kissed her, their lips felt as if they had been made to fit together.

And in bed, their bodies were so in sync, it was crazy. Teddy knew exactly how to hold her, to not treat her like some fragile thing, to really fuck her until they were both exhausted. And she couldn't get enough of him, and they would make love long into the night, even when she had to be in court early the next morning.

Her friends—especially the conspirators India and Coco—were delighted for her, and Massimo and Teddy were fast becoming friends, which made the upcoming film they were making together all the more exciting.

It felt like more than two lifetimes since that first night and now and when she saw his name pop up on her phone later that morning, her chest warmed at the sound of his voice. "Hey, gorgeous."

"Hey yourself. Filming stopped?"

"In between takes. They're setting up. Listen, Dorcas

just called. Apparently DJ is sick, so she can't visit with me today." He sounded a little pissed, and Jess wondered if he'd argued with Dorcas.

"Well, if she's sick... listen, we're still going ahead with the move for joint custody, so if Dorcas is playing around, she won't be able to do it for long. And DJ may actually be sick. It's not like Dorcas would lie about that, surely? I mean, I'm not a parent, but it would seem to me..."

"You're right," Teddy interjected. "I'm just being paranoid."

"You okay?"

He gave a sheepish laugh. "Like I said, paranoia. But what after Dorcas has pulled before, nothing she could do would surprise me." He let out a breath, clearly relaxing. "Listen... can I persuade you to play hooky tonight?

"You can... want to come to my place? I can cook."

Teddy chuckled. "Of course you can, you're Superwoman."

"Ha, believe me, I'm not, but keep thinking that way, I like it. Come by whenever you want, I'll be home after six."

"I can't wait."

Coco shifted uncomfortably in her seat and studied her friend. India was bent over her laptop, typing furiously, her brow furrowed, and Coco noticed that she kept wincing and holding her side. "Boo, you okay?"

India looked up, blinking as if surprised that Coco was

in the room. She always got absorbed when she was writing. "Just some nerve pain."

"Do you want some pain killers?"

"Trying not to succumb. I got way too dependent on the Vicodin after the stabbing. It kind of scared me how much I relied on them. So, no thanks. I'll ride it out."

Coco nodded. "Fine but let me make you some tea at least."

India grinned at her. "You're mothering me. I should be pampering you; you're the preggo one."

"Pah." Coco got up, nevertheless placing her hand over her small bump. "Piece of cake so far."

India followed her into the kitchen. "I always meant to say, I think it's a great thing you and Alex are doing. I know Alex has wanted a kid for years. This makes sense."

"Thanks, boo. I have to admit I'm excited." She nodded at India. "It'll be your turn next."

India flushed a little, and Coco wondered if she'd hit a nerve. "Have you and Massimo talked about it?"

Indy nodded. "We have, at various points and for a couple of months now. We've been, let's just say, *casual* with birth control. But—" She hesitated and sighed. "But if I'm honest… I'm not even sure I want kids."

That shocked Coco. "Really? I mean, having kids is not an imperative for everyone, but… well, I just assumed. I shouldn't have, I'm sorry. Is this to do with your daughter?"

India nodded. "Yes, and to be honest, she isn't my daughter. We only share DNA, and you and I both know that means nothing... hopefully it means very little to her, given who her father was."

"I never told you how proud I was with you for going ahead with that pregnancy after everything. For not blaming the child for how she was conceived. A family is happy because of your bravery."

"I'm *not* brave," India said suddenly, her eyes filling with tears, "I feel like the biggest coward on Earth."

Coco wrapped her arms around her distressed friend. "What is it, Indy? You haven't been yourself this whole visit."

"I ran away," India sobbed, "From Massimo, from Sun when he needed me. And I caused so much pain... I can't bear it. Everyone has been so kind, but I want someone to get angry with me, to shout and scream at me that I was irresponsible... stupid, stupid woman." She was crying hard now, and Coco held onto her tightly.

"Oh, sweetheart."

"Don't be nice to me, it makes it worse."

Coco pursed her lips. "Fine. Look at me." India, her cheeks tear-streaked and bright pink, did as she was told. "Just stop it. Stop feeling guilty; stop feeling sorry for yourself. Yes, you could have handled things differently, but it is what it is. Carter is dead. You got a knife stuck in your gut *again*. You almost died. Sun almost died. But both of you *survived*. Nothing is easy, nothing is straightforward. The circumstances were exceptional; none of us were thinking straight. So stop with the guilt. It's done." Her eyes softened, and she stroked a strand of India's hair back from her damp face. "And sweetheart, you need to talk to someone. A professional. I've thought it for a while, and I know it's been on Massi's mind."

India wiped her eyes on the sleeve of her sweater. "He's talked about it?"

"He wasn't going behind your back; he just worries."

India sighed. "I know. But, honestly, I feel kind of pathetic, and I'm scared he'll get tired of it."

"That man loves you with all his heart, Indy."

India half-smiled. "I know that, too." She grabbed a tissue from the box on the counter and blew her nose loudly. "I'm a mess."

"Kinda."

India laughed. "Look, I'm sick of being stuck inside. Let's go shopping for your bambino."

10
CHAPTER TEN – MAKE ME FEEL

Jess was closing her laptop just before six p.m. when Bee knocked on her door. "Jess? It's online."

It took Jess a moment to remember about the 'exposé,' but she just shrugged. "I'll take a look later. Seriously, Bee, don't worry about it. I'm not."

She drove home, almost immediately forgetting about the exposé, trying to figure out what groceries she had in her meagre refrigerator. She was ashamed—and amused—to realize she'd never cooked for a date before; even Margot had always been the one to make their food.

And it wasn't as if she didn't love to cook; even in college, she and India had taken classes together, learning the finer points of *cordon bleu* cuisine, but Jess hadn't continued cooking after that time as India had.

She swung into Whole Foods and picked up some fresh chicken and vegetables and a handful of fresh rosemary and thyme. At home, she rubbed butter infused with the herbs and some garlic all over the chicken and shoved half a lemon into the chicken's cavity before putting it into the oven. Simple, she thought, but always, always good. She chopped up some vegetables to roast and set them aside for later.

Her phone bleeped, and she saw a message from Teddy. *On my way...*

Jess grinned, typing back *You better be, I'm all naked and soaped up...*

She went to her bedroom and stripped off, going into the shower and cranking on the faucet. She stood under the spray and slowly soaped her body, enjoying the self-massage. She heard his car on the gravel driveway to her home and grinned to herself.

She'd left a note on the door... Come on in, take it all off...

She heard his chuckle as he came into the bathroom and saw her in the shower. "Wow. You sure know how to greet a fella."

Jess slid open the glass door. "Quiet, boy, and get in here."

Teddy, grinning widely, tugged off his sweater and dropped his pants, kicking his sneakers off. Naked, he slid into the cubicle with her and slid his arms around her. "Hey, beautiful."

"Hey yourself." Jess pressed her lips against his, and they kissed slowly, enjoying the taste of feel of each other. She could feel his cock, hard and straining, standing proud against her belly. "Wanna put that in me?"

"Like you wouldn't believe…"

He lifted her out of the shower and carried her to her bed still wet, and Jess plucked a condom from her drawer and rolled it down his cock. Teddy hitched her legs around his waist and thrust into her. "God, Jess, you feel so good…"

She smiled up at him, tightening her vagina around his pumping cock, feeling every inch of him as he fucked her. "Fuck me hard, Theodore."

He laughed. "As you wish, my lady."

They made love, laughing and joking around, but also with a tenderness that Jess hadn't known she was capable of. She loved being in this man's arms, love the scratch of his beard against her face—and on her thighs when he went down on her, which he loved doing. Hell, Jess didn't argue with that, Teddy Hood's tongue was the stuff of legend.

Eventually, Jess remembered about the roast chicken and got up in a hurry to rescue it. Teddy, tugging on his clothes, followed her into the chicken. "That smells divine."

Over dinner and a really good bottle of wine, they chatted, and Jess was glad to see that Teddy had let the whole cancelled plans with DJ thing go. Teddy called his daughter after dinner to say goodnight and reported that DJ was feeling better. "She's going back to school tomorrow, so we're going out afterward."

He looked so happy that Jess couldn't help but smile. She gathered up their plates and headed to the kitchen.

Looking out of the window, she frowned. A news van was parked on the sidewalk outside her house, and as she watched, two more turned up. "What the fuck?"

"What is it?"

"Network news is on my lawn."

Teddy came to stand beside her, but she pushed him a little away. "Don't let them see you. It'll be like chum in the water. What the hell is this about?"

"Want me to get rid of them?"

Jess shook her head. "No, I don't want them to know you're here." She realized she might have sounded rude and smiled ruefully at him. "Not that I'm ashamed of us, far from it, but we don't want to give Dorcas any reason to bitch."

"Understood."

"I'm going to go out and see what this is about?"

Jess tugged open her front door to see one of the journalists and his camera crew descending on her. She carefully closed the door behind her. "Hey fellas, what gives?"

"Hey, Jess, you got any comment?"

"On what?" She was genuinely confused, and she saw the reporter and cameraman exchange glances. "Out with it, guys. I'm a big girl, I can handle it."

"You must know about Taran Googe?"

"He's a YouTuber, right? Ah..." Realization dawned, and she smiled. "Yes, I heard something about him doing an exposé on me. Good luck finding anything, Mr. Googe."

The reporter colored a little. "Jess... he's dragged up the whole Simon Lamont thing."

"What Simon Lamont thing? Simon is the lawyer who gave me my first break in law, yes, but I haven't seen or spoken to him in years. I know he was named in a sexual harassment suit last year, and although I don't know the facts of the case, he was found guilty by a jury of his peers. So, how does that affect me?"

"Googe is alleging you got where you did by, um, exchanging favors of work."

Jess rolled her eyes. "And for that, they send you out here? Guys, you know how many times a man has taken credit for my work? Or for my success? Daily, fellas, daily. It happens to all women, and more often than not, they think we whore ourselves out for work. My law degree says otherwise. So... a pissant little twerp like Taran Googe can say what he wants. None of it is true."

Again that look between the two men, and Jess started to get annoyed. "What?"

"Jess, Googe talked to your father. He more or less confirmed what Googe said."

Ouch. *Ouch.* "Well, seeing as I haven't seen or talked to my father in seventeen years, and that's way before I even met Simon Lamont, he wouldn't know anything about me, my work, or my life. So... no story here, I'm sorry. Goodnight, fellas."

SHE WENT BACK INSIDE, irked, irritated and when Teddy saw her face, he went to her immediately. "What is it?"

"Nothing big, just an annoying pseudo-journalist calling me a whore on the internet."

Teddy frowned and steered her into a chair. "Tell me."

So she did, and by the time she had finished, Teddy was incensed on her behalf. Jess put her hand on his leg. "Teddy, there's no point in being pissed off. This stuff is bull crap, it'll blow over."

BUT THEY SOON DISCOVERED IT would be more than just a passing annoyance. To Teddy's annoyance, Dorcas was on it straight away, retweeting the links to the video and posting cryptic, passive aggressive jibes about 'her ex-husband's choice of lawyer.'

But she made no attempt to stop Teddy seeing DJ... yet. Jess found some of Teddy's paranoia catching, wondering if she should recuse herself from the case but Teddy wouldn't hear of it. "You're the reason she ran scared and let me see DJ. You are my last hope, Obi Wan."

Jess snickered. "You are such a dork, Teddy Hood." She perched on his lap. "What would the paying public think of their number one movie stud being such a geek?"

"I think they know."

"Uh-oh. No more *People's Sexiest Man* awards for you. It's all *Gaming Weekly*."

"Have you ever read a gaming magazine in your life?" Teddy was stroking her back, grinning up at her.

"No, because I'm not a dork and I *have* seen a lady naked."

Teddy snorted. "Snob."

"You know it." Jess sighed. "Maybe we should watch it, so we know what we're dealing with. If the press keep coming by, they'll catch you one of these days."

Teddy shrugged. "Maybe we should. Although I don't care who knows about us, I really don't. I want the whole world to know that I got so lucky this time around."

That got to Jess, and she smiled at him. "That's such a sweet thing to say."

"I'm just saying it to get into your pants." Teddy wiggled his eyebrows at her mischievously.

"I should hope so." But she kissed him fiercely. "Let's watch this nonsense, then forget about it."

"Deal."

Taran Googe was a deeply unattractive man, both physically and personally, Teddy decided a half hour later as they watched his documentary. *If you can call it that. This is a hack job,* Teddy shook his head. It pained him to see Jess so denigrated after everything she had gone through to get where she was in her life. She sat silently watching the show, her face impassive, but Teddy knew her enough by now to know that when she got quiet, it meant she was either angry or upset.

Probably both. He slid his hand onto the back of her neck and massaged it gently. "Remember it's bullshit."

"I am." But her eyes changed as an older man came onto the screen, and Teddy realized this was her estranged father.

"No, it doesn't surprise me that Jessica got mixed up

with someone like Simon Lamont. She was always ruthless in all of her dealings," her father told Taran with obvious relish. "She's one of those women who don't know when to shut up and sit down. Pushy. A real ballbuster."

"And this dude is your father?"

"India's dad tried to have her murdered. Twice. I got it easy with this asshole." She said it calmly, but he felt the tension rolling off her. He picked up the remote and flicked the television off.

"I want to see the rest," Jess said, but Teddy shook his head.

"Later. Right now, we're going to talk."

Jess sighed. "Look, okay... yes, it hurts. But it's heresay, and even if people believe it, so what? I'm still the best divorce lawyer in this town and people know it. Who cares if I fucked my way to the top? And by the way, I didn't."

Teddy smiled at her. "You don't have to tell me that, baby."

Jess's eyes softened. "I know. I needed to say it aloud, though."

He stroked her cheek. "You can rant and rave at me all you want. This loser—" he nodded at the now quiet television, "—I swear to God, he's like one of those kids in the schoolyard, pinching and poking at a girl because he likes her."

Jess rolled her eyes. "Not everyone wants to sleep with me, Teddy."

"Wanna bet?"

"Ha ha. Look, let's forget it for now. Like I said, this

idiot can bawl and whine, but it'll go nowhere if I don't react. He wants a reaction, you're right about that, but he has nothing." Jess leaned over and kissed him. "Take me to bed, Hood."

THEY MADE love long into the night, but when Teddy had fallen asleep, Jess found the same sleep evading her. She got up and went to the kitchen, grabbing some milk from the fridge. She knew what was bothering her.

Her dad. She'd always been scared of him growing up; his fragile masculinity was threatened by his two daughters, Jess and her younger sister Katie, both of whom excelled in school and in college. Their mother, Therese, had been a professor, something that had always rankled Ian Olden, the thought that his wife was not only a noted beauty, but intelligent. He'd been able to destroy her confidence enough, but his daughters had seen what he did and wouldn't allow the same thing to happen to them. Jess, in particular, had rebelled. She didn't take a penny of his money to put herself through school, and after Katie had died...

God, it still hurt so much. Katie was always sunshine and rainbows, and no one saw her suicide coming. No one. *Not even me*, Jess thought, miserable even now. *How? Why?*

After Katie's funeral, she'd returned to college, and the next day at the student bar, she'd met a girl who looked as devastated as she felt. India and Jess were inseparable from that day, their shared pain giving way to a deep abiding friendship.

God, she was getting maudlin, and when she got down, she found it increasingly hard to see the good side of things. *Nope, not gonna be that girl.*

Especially not now with Teddy. As soon as she thought of the man in her bed, her spirits lifted. That was who mattered now. Not her dad. Not some pissant dweeb on the internet. She checked out of the window, and saw the news crews had departed. She still couldn't believe they'd sent a team out for this.

But then again... Simon Lamont's trial was coming up and they probably needed b-roll for something. God. She had never told anyone about her experience with Lamont. It wasn't something she even wanted to think about. Needless to say, she believed the women who had accused her former boss.

"Yo, your honor, coming back to bed soon?"

She turned and grinned at a very disheveled Teddy standing in the doorway, smiling at her in a way that made her stomach warm and desire curl through her. "Hmm, let me see... I could... or you could fuck me here on the cold kitchen tile."

There was a beat of silence, then Jess shrieked with laughter as Teddy chased her around the breakfast bar before tackling her to the floor, kissing her and gathering her in his arms. "I'm crazy about you, Jessica Olden."

"Right back at you, Theodore. Kiss me again... and again... and *again*..."

CHAPTER ELEVEN – BREATHE

Dorcas listened to what her private detective told her calmly, then thanked him, handed him his check, and excused him. Then, she went upstairs to her room, closed the door, and screamed, ranting and raving, throwing things, breaking glass.

Downstairs in the kitchen, her daughter cast a look at Johanna, who placed a hand on DJ's back. "It's okay, sweetie."

DJ sighed. "I know. I think Mommy just found out that Daddy's got a new girlfriend."

"He has?"

DJ nodded. "He told me about her last week. I think he loves her because when he was talking about her, his face went all... soft."

Johanna chuckled. "Soft?"

"Like this." DJ made her expression dreamy and

Johanna laughed. "He had heart eyes for her," DJ explained.

"Well, good. Right?"

DJ nodded enthusiastically. "Right."

"Shouldn't you be getting ready for school?"

Neither had seen Dorcas, recovered from her quick temper tantrum, standing in the doorway watching them. Johanna colored and turned away, and DJ slid from her chair. "I'll get my books."

"I'll take DJ to school today, Johanna," Dorcas said steadily, her anger simmering below the surface, but all too evident to Johanna who had known the family for years. Luckily for her, she was indispensable—and she knew way too much about Dorcas for Dorcas to fire her.

Johanna got DJ's lunch out of the refrigerator, but Dorcas grabbed the box and turned away without another word.

IN THE CAR on the way to school, Dorcas looked in the rearview at her daughter sitting patiently and quietly in the backseat. "So... you know Daddy has a new girlfriend."

"Yes, Mommy."

Dorcas's mouth tightened. "Have you met her?"

"No. Not yet."

"Not yet."

"No."

Dorcas struggled to rein in her temper. Jessica Fucking

Olden. She had suspected Teddy was fucking her, but to have it confirmed... "Has Daddy talked about her?"

"Some." Jesus, getting any information out of DJ was going to be a long, drawn-out battle, she could tell. No matter, DJ would be useful in other ways.

Dorcas handed DJ her lunch pack as she dropped her off. "I want you to eat it all today, no leftovers. I put your favorites in."

DJ looked skeptical but nodded and disappeared into the pack of friends she had waiting for her. Dorcas watched her daughter chatting animatedly with her friends and wondered at her easy way of drawing people to her, Dorcas never had that gift, even as a child. She'd always had to use her beauty to get what she wanted. She glanced in the rearview again, this time at her own reflection. She was rail-thin now, but all she could see was the sharp, fragile beauty of her youth. It was only in her eyes that she saw what she had become.

She slipped her sunglasses on and pulled her car away from the school and into traffic. She pondered going to Jess Olden's house, seeing if she could catch Teddy coming out of her place... but that would mean admitting she was having him followed. That she was having Jess investigated.

Fuck. She pounded the steering wheel in frustration. If Jess Olden thought she could take her husband and her daughter away, she had another think coming.

Still, she had already put into the motion the plan that would get Teddy running back to her.

Dorcas drove home and waited all day for the phone call from the school telling her that her daughter was sick.

Venice

MASSIMO HAD SURPRISED India with a trip back to Venice where they had first met on the anniversary of that beautiful night. They stayed in the penthouse suite of Venice's best hotel, and although they were both looking forward to exploring the city again, they spent the first afternoon in their suite.

Eventually, though, they were starving and went out to eat at one of their favorite restaurants. Massimo ordered a bottle of champagne and toasted his fiancée. India looked particularly beautiful tonight, he thought, her caramel skin in a gold dress, her lovely face more relaxed than he had seen in months.

She had been seeing a therapist in New York, and although the first few weeks had been rough, he had noticed a definite improvement in her mood, and it filled him with joy. He had his Indy back, after everything.

"Bella, you have never looked more beautiful than you do tonight."

India flushed—really, the woman could not take a compliment—and kissed him. "I love you so much, my Italian king."

He chuckled. "Well, only a king would be worthy of you."

India stroked his cheek. "I'm sorry I put you through hell, baby. I'm so sorry."

"Stop apologizing for something out of your control. I would go through hell for you every minute if I had to…" He swallowed, remembering suddenly the terrifying, devastating sight of her in the hospital, barely alive, when he didn't know if she would ever open those beautiful eyes of hers again and tell him she loved him…

"Baby?"

He blinked. "Sorry, darling, I was just…"

"You went pale."

He waved his hand. "It was nothing, I promise. Let's enjoy our meal."

But through the meal, that image of India so hurt, so brutalized, haunted him, and it affected the mood of the evening. India looked at him, and he could see the confusion in her eyes. "Talk to me, Massi."

"It truly is nothing, my sweet baby. Let's just enjoy the evening."

As they walked through the night streets of Venice, over the small bridges, watching the boats on the Grand Canal, Massimo held India's hand, and she nudged his shoulder with hers, smiling up at him. "This will always be our place," she said softly, "the place where we met, then met again, and where we made love for the first time. Where we made love on camera for all the world to see."

Massimo smiled at the memory. They had filmed a music video for a hot single of India's, and during a love scene, had actually made love. The record had been a worldwide sensation, as had the music video, and the rumors had swirled about the sex scene, but it was their secret. They both enjoyed the tease, however.

India suddenly pulled him into an alleyway, deserted and dark, and pushed him against the stone wall of a building. She pressed her lips to his fiercely, and the mood took him, running his hands down her body, between her legs, hearing her soft moan of desire. His cock responded immediately.

"*Bellisimo* India, if I'm not inside you in the next few minutes, I might go mad."

She took his hand and they ran over a couple of bridges to reach their hotel.

Inside, they wasted no time tearing each other's clothes off, and India gasped as he hitched her legs around his waist. "Forgive me, India, but I cannot wait…"

She grinned breathless. "Good…fuck me, Massimo, fuck me hard…please…"

His cock, thick and long, plunged deep into her, and she cried out at the quick pain. Massimo hesitated but she nodded at him eagerly. "Harder baby, *harder…*"

And he obliged, plowing his cock deep into her cunt, pinning her hands to the floor with his, telling her to look at him, his eyes boring into hers as he fucked her. God, the feel of him as he rammed his hips against hers, the way he filled her entirely, dominating her body.

"God, India, beautiful, beautiful India, I'm going to fuck you every way this night, I swear I am...*sei una dea, sei una dea.*" *You are a Goddess.*

He made her come not once, but twice, before he climaxed, shooting thick, creamy cum deep inside her, then began his assault on every one of her senses, biting down then sucking her nipples, rimming her navel with his tongue. When his mouth found her sex, he heard her moan and felt her writhe beneath him.

She was his, only his, and no one else could touch them in this moment. Massimo's entire concentration was on the beautiful woman in his arms, his Indy, the girl who had survived so much, and yet somehow still just wanted his love to make her happy.

"*Ti amo*, India Blue," he murmured as he made his way back to her mouth, his lips fixing on her soft skin.

They came together, sighing and panting for air as they collapsed together on the bed. Soon, India was asleep in his arms, and he kissed her closed eyelids gently and tried to sleep himself.

THE NIGHTMARES BEGAN, and he was like a voyeur, calling out to India as she stepped into her old Venice apartment. She didn't respond, and he realized he was no more than a ghost...

. . .

India shook out her soaking wet hair as she opened the door to her apartment, then, looking down, realized the rain shower had soaked her white dress, making it both see through, and cling to her skin. *Thank God, I wore underwear,* she grinned to herself and, went to her bedroom to grab a towel.

As she stepped through the door, she saw a movement to her side, but before she could react, someone grabbed her. She struggled and kicked out, panicked, and managed to free herself and get to the kitchen before she was brought down to the floor. Her attacker flipped her onto her back, then another man dropped onto her legs, pinning her, as a hand was clamped over her mouth. India looked up into the eyes of the man who had stabbed her all those years ago and knew she was going to die, and no one could save her.

Massimo signed some autographs, cursing that he hadn't waited until the middle of the night to fly to Venice. He just couldn't be away from India a moment more.

"Hey, Massimo! You going to marry India?"

Massimo, scrawling his signature on outstretched magazines, shot the journalist an incredulous look. "Of course I am... she's the love of my life."

The photographers went mad then, and he had to fight to get through the throng to his car. Sighing gratefully as the car pulled away, and he was travelling, he thought about what he had just told the press.

It was true. India was the love of his life, there was no argument, and he had been a fool to let her leave that hotel room *thinking otherwise. He couldn't wait to see her, kiss her, tell her he was so Goddamned in love with her that it was painful, that he could not imagine life without her. If she forgave him, if she'd let him, he would take her straight to city hall and marry her then and there. Tomorrow. Hell, tonight...he was sure he could arrange it. Then he'd take her down to his island, and they would spend days, weeks, even months, fucking and loving and laughing.*

He leaned forward and spoke to the driver. "Please, hurry. I need to get to my love."

Braydon smiled down at India and ran a fingertip down her stomach until it rested in her navel. "As beautiful as ever, my darling India. Oh, where are my manners? This is Zeke. I brought him along because he wanted to watch me kill you. Say hello, Zeke."

Zeke grinned down at her nastily, his big, rough hand still clamped over her mouth.

Braydon was admiring her body, visible through the drenched dress. "Sweet India...it was always going to end this way, you know? My knife in your belly." He brought out a stiletto knife from his pocket, and India watched in disbelief as he raised it above his head. His gaze was almost loving. "I've dreamed of this moment for a decade, beautiful one."

And he slammed the blade deep into her navel again and again. India couldn't believe the agony. The hand was lifted from her face as Braydon stabbed her, but she couldn't scream, couldn't catch her breath.

"Boss..." She heard Zeke's plaintive cry and wondered if he was telling Braydon that was enough. Braydon stopped then and grinned.

"Where are my manners? Of course..." He handed the knife to Zeke. For a second, India wondered if it was over, but that hope was horrifically dashed a second later when Braydon added, "Just in her belly, Zeke."

Zeke stabbed her again, giggling like a child as he drove the blade deep into her ruined belly.

"God..." she whispered as she felt herself losing consciousness, "Massimo..."

"Stop," said Braydon, and Zeke let go of the knife, the hilt still protruding from India's body. "She'll never survive this. It is done."

He leaned over and kissed her mouth. "Goodbye, my darling one. I finished what I started...and before you die, know this. A decade ago? When I killed your mother and fucked you? Your father paid me to do it. He wanted you both dead, and he didn't care how I did it. When I saw the photograph he gave me of you, I've never felt so exhilarated—to know I could take you, and fuck you, and then put my knife in you. In the end, he paid me, and I did exactly what I wanted. That's why he wouldn't testify against me, India, because he knew I would rat him out in a heartbeat."

He stroked her face as she struggled to breathe, the agony and the blood loss making her head whirl. "That I decided to finish it now is just my reward. He told me where you were living here in Venice." He leaned in closer, his lips at her ear. "I told him I was going to kill you...do you know what he said,

India? He told me to do it. Your own father. Die knowing that, beautiful girl."

He got up and nodded to Zeke who let go of India. She couldn't move, near death now, and her eyes closed as she heard the door slam behind her killers.

Massimo got *out of the water taxi and a sense of rightness came over him. He looked up at the open shutters of her little apartment—the place where they had fallen in love—and his heart swelled. He took the stairs two at a time and knocked on her door. No answer.*

"Bella? Sweet baby? It's me, Massimo. Please let me in. I know you're in there, your windows are open."

Again, no answer, and Massimo began to get nervous. "India, please. I know you're mad, I know I hurt you, but you have to know...nothing happened between Valentina and I. Nothing. It would never happen, because I love you and you alone. You are the reason I breathe in and out."

Massimo listened for any movement inside but heard nothing. He sighed and took a step back from the door, closing his eyes, his head dropping. He rubbed his eyes then, and when he opened them, he saw it.

Blood. Pooling out from under the door. Adrenaline and horror flooded his system. "India! No, no, please...someone help please!"

He threw himself against the door over and over until it gave in, and as he almost fell inside the room, he saw her.

The shock was icy cold. India lay, soaked in blood, the hilt of a knife protruding from her belly. Her white dress was scarlet with her blood, her eyes closed. She looked so pale. Massimo's legs gave way, and he had to crawl to her, taking her head onto his lap, bending to hear if she was still breathing, the scream he heard was coming from his soul, a desiccating howl of grief.

"No! India, no! Please! Live..." But she lay limp in his arms, and when he pressed his fingers to her throat to find a pulse, there was none. He sobbed, screaming, and when he looked up, her eyes were open, accusing.

"You couldn't save me, Massimo... you could never have saved me..."

MASSIMO WOKE IN A COLD SWEAT, calling out her name.

CHAPTER TWELVE – HUMBLE

Los Angeles

JESS HAD a longstanding invitation to her actor friend Seth Mackenzie's party, and it was way too late to duck out, so when she found herself at his place in the Hollywood Hills, she told herself it was a half-hour thing, and then she'd escape.

Teddy was also out this evening, supporting a fellow actor friend at a premiere, and so she was flying solo at the party. Luckily she saw quite a few friends there, and her half-hour thing ended up being more like the entire evening.

She was thinking about making her escape when she saw him and almost laughed. Taran Googe was standing in the corner of the room, people-watching, nursing a drink. He was smaller in person than he made himself look on the internet, and there was a weaselly-creepiness to him that made her lip curl in distaste.

Jess snagged Seth's arm as he passed by. "Seth… what the hell is that Googe loser doing at one of your parties?"

Seth looked over and shrugged. "Someone must have brought him as their plus-one." Realization dawned on his handsome face. "Oh, lord… look, I'll get someone to throw him out, Jess."

"No, don't bother. This is where I get to have my fun." Jess gave a wicked smile, ready to confront the man who had made an effort to bring her down. To let him know he had in no way *succeeded* in doing so.

Seth shrugged and kissed her cheek. "Have at him. Just don't break any of my stuff."

Jess snorted as Seth moved away, and then she very deliberately went up to the bar where Googe stood. Out of the corner of her eye, she saw him start with surprise when he recognized her.

"Well, if it isn't Jessica Olden."

Jess smoothed out her expression and turned to him, her eyes cold. "I'm sorry, have we met?"

"You know who I am, Ms. Olden."

Wow. "You'll have to remind me."

She saw a faint flicker of doubt in his eyes. God, he was repellent. A faint sheen of sweat hung on his upper lip, his eyes were a dirty grey, his red hair short, his face unshaven.

A faint stink of tobacco wafted off of his skin. "Taran Googe."

"Should I know who you are, Mr. Googe?"

He grinned nastily. "You should. I just released a documentary about you."

"About me? What on earth could be so interesting about me?" Jess was enjoying herself now. What a little squirt this dude was.

"Jess, come on, now. Your past with Simon Lamont, your dealings with Teddy Hood."

"My 'dealings'? Mr. Hood is my client, Mr. Googe, and Simon Lamont was my old employer. So?"

He smirked, and Jess resisted the temptation to smack him right in the middle of his smug face. The way he looked at her body also made her temper roil, but she kept it in check. Don't hand him a victory.

"Now that I'm meeting you in person," he breathed on her, "I'm beginning to regret my angle. How about we go somewhere private and discuss it?"

Was he kidding? Where the fuck did he get his lines from, a cheesy 80s movie? Jess met his gaze with an icy cold glare. "Listen, *boy*, I want you to enjoy your day in the sun. Take a good look around because this is your one shot at this, okay? Uploading crap isn't going to cut it much longer; you're actually going to have to create something worth the status."

Taran Googe was still grinning. "So you did see it."

"Of course I did. I watched it, and then you know what I did? I forgot about it because it was all bullshit. But you know that already, don't you? You're just a hack looking for a way to make a quick buck." Jess smiled coldly at him. Taran Googe wasn't smiling anymore, and there was a small crowd of people watching them—all of them friends of Jess.

Jess hadn't finished with him yet. "And don't come on to me like some ignorant schoolboy. Don't insinuate that you'd retract your crappy documentary if I were to 'service' you. It's disgusting—not to mention amateur."

Taran, his face red, turned and walked out of the party. A small cheer went up around Jess. "God, I love it when you're masterful," Seth hooked his arm across Jess's shoulders. "Tell me again why you're not a professional dominatrix?"

Jess grinned. "You wish."

"That little drip was sleazing on me earlier," another actress she vaguely recognized said with a shudder. "Who let him in?"

Jess left them to try and figure out which among them had brought the interloper. She thanked Seth for the invite and escaped thankfully to where her car was parked. Just as she touched the door handle, she noticed it.

Bitch

Keyed into the paintwork of her Mercedes. Nice... and dumb. Seth's place had security cameras out the wazoo—maybe Taran Googe just didn't care that they would know it was him. Dude was an amateur.

Strangely, Jess was amused by the incident rather than pissed. It just confirmed to her that Taran Googe had no idea what he was doing, and that she really did have nothing to worry about.

She drove home to find Teddy already at her place. It was weird to think that they had fallen into sharing their homes as if they always had—she had a key to his apartment and he one to her condo, and that's just the way it was.

TEDDY OPENED the door for her as Jess approached and took her in his arms. He really couldn't get enough of this gorgeous woman. "How was the party?"

"Better than expected—and I got an added bonus."

Jess told him about her encounter with Googe. "Seriously, the dude's a moron. Building up all that supposed credibility, then blowing it all on a crass come-on." Jess laughed, and Teddy was glad to see she wasn't taking Googe at all seriously—not that she had anyway. Jess was remarkably sanguine when it came to attacks on her character, he realized, her self-confidence not knocked by much. He loved that about her.

He loved *her*.

He'd known it for a while now, but hadn't plucked up the courage to tell her, which he knew would seem ridiculous to most people. He was Teddy Hood, Hollywood movie star, eligible bachelor, and now he was soft on a girl. He felt like a teenager around her, and even sometimes, he felt... not exactly inferior, but Jess had a strength that he hadn't seen in any woman he had dated before. He found it wildly alluring and irresistible.

It was already after midnight and they went to bed, making love slowly, enjoying the sensations of each other's hands on their skin before falling asleep.

It was almost four a.m. when Dorcas called Teddy to tell him that DJ was in the hospital again.

CHAPTER THIRTEEN – WIRES

Los Angeles

TEDDY TRIED to tamp down the panic as he and Jess ran through the hospital corridors to the emergency room. When he saw Dorcas, no make-up and tear-stained, his heart missed a beat. *Please God, no...*

"Dorcas? Where's DJ?"

"They're doing some tests. She won't stop throwing up, and she's complaining of a terrible headache. She's been sick for hours, and I don't know what to do."

Teddy breathed out. "Jesus, Dorcas, why didn't you call me earlier?"

"If I called you every time DJ threw up lately, you'd accuse me of stalking you." Dorcas cut her eyes at Jess, and she gave a humorless smirk. "You bring your divorce lawyer to the hospital? How classy and yet staggeringly inappropriate."

Teddy didn't answer her, and Jess looked uncomfortable. "Why don't I go get us all some coffee?"

"Yes, why don't you?" Dorcas' tone was dismissive, and Teddy felt a wave of annoyance. But now was not the time for a fight. Jess squeezed his shoulder, then disappeared. Teddy looked at Dorcas. "Tell me everything. What do you mean DJ's been throwing up a lot lately? Why don't I know about this?"

"DJ didn't tell you? Interesting."

Teddy let his annoyance show at the jibe. "Now is not the time for point scoring, Dorcas. What the fuck is wrong with you?"

Dorcas opened her mouth to speak, but they were interrupted by the doctor who came out of the room opposite. "You can see DJ now. We've given her an anti-emetic and some painkillers. She's groggy but awake." He looked at Teddy and smiled kindly. "She's been asking for you."

"Doctor, what's wrong with her?" Dorcas sounded more annoyed than worried, and Teddy shot her a warning look.

"We don't know for sure. We've taken some bloods, and we'll run a toxicology profile. Those results will take a while to come back. It could just be stomach flu; that's the most likely cause of her illness. Kids pick up a myriad of bugs at school, but with DJ's history... we'll be better off making sure."

"There are no drugs at all in *my* house," Dorcas said stiffly, and Teddy rolled his eyes. *Sure, Jan.*

"Nor mine," he said smoothly, smiling at the doctor. "DJ's been doing really well these days. I'm sure it is just stomach flu."

TEDDY WENT into see his daughter and tried not to look shocked at how pale she was. Still, she gave him a bright smile. "Hey, Dad."

"Hey little dude." He high-fived her. "So, you're a Yak Monster, huh?"

"It's so gross," DJ said, giggling at his nickname for her, "but I feel better now you're here." She looked behind him, and it seemed to Teddy she was looking hopeful about something. DJ leaned into him. "You on your own?" Casually asked, but he could see the curiosity in her eyes.

Teddy smiled. "No, Jess is with me."

"And you left her with *Mom*?" DJ's eyes grew big, and Teddy couldn't help but laugh.

"Believe me, Jess can hold her own." Teddy swept his hand onto his daughter's forehead. "Mom tells me you've been sick a lot lately."

"Some. My stomach hurts."

Teddy studied her. "DJ… you know you can tell me anything, right? Anything. If something is making you unhappy…"

"I promise, Daddy. I didn't take anything this time."

Her eyes were big and earnest, and Teddy nodded, believing her.

"Then it's probably just a stomach flu, kiddo. It means you get a few days ditching school. Yay?"

DJ giggled. "Yay... kinda." She sighed, seeming a hundred times older than her eight years. "It means Mommy will play nursemaid again. She won't leave me alone."

Teddy nodded, careful not to let his irritation with Dorcas show. It wasn't justified in this case—she had every right and every reason to fuss over DJ like this, and Teddy had to hand it to her, she had really stepped up this time.

"Knock, knock." Dorcas came into the room. She handed DJ a cup of ice chips. "Darling, you look a little better."

"I'm okay, Mommy."

Dorcas perched on the edge of the bed. "You always seem brighter when the three of us are together," she said, casually, and stroked her daughter's hair. "Perhaps Daddy would like to come to dinner with us when you're feeling better?"

Teddy shot Dorcas a look, but he didn't want to question her sudden benevolence in front of DJ. "How about it, kiddo?"

"Can Jess come?"

Dorcas's eyes flashed with anger. "I don't think that would be appropriate, do you? She's your Daddy's lawyer."

Teddy knew for sure then that Dorcas knew about him and Jess. He could see it in her face. He wondered if

Dorcas was having him followed, and then realized that was exactly what she was doing. Still, right now, he didn't care about that. DJ was his priority. He smiled at his daughter. "Would you like to meet Jess?" He wasn't *that* magnanimous that he could resist a little dig at his ex-wife.

DJ nodded, smiling widely, and Teddy got up. "I'll go get her."

Dorcas followed him out. "What the hell are you doing?"

"Introducing my girlfriend to my daughter," Teddy replied smoothly, "but you know that already, don't you, Dorcas?"

Dorcas's eyes narrowed. "Fucking your lawyer. How classy of both you."

"As classy as having me investigated? Pot, let me introduce you to kettle." Teddy was aware his voice was rising and sighed. "This isn't the time nor place."

"To introduce your fuck buddy to our sick daughter? I agree. Get rid of her." Dorcas went back into DJ's room, leaving Teddy shaking his head.

"Hey."

He turned to see Jess behind him, and he smiled at her. "Hey. Did you overhear that?"

"Yup. She's right, though, this isn't the time nor place. Look, I'm going to go, give you some space. You need to be with your daughter right now." Jess kissed him softly. "This isn't me running away. Let's just do things right. The last thing DJ needs is her parent's fighting. I'll be waiting when you're ready. I'm glad she's okay."

Teddy leaned his forehead against hers. "Thank you for being here for me."

"You're welcome." She pressed her lips to his, quickly but tenderly. "Call me if you need anything."

Teddy watched her walk away and wondered why he couldn't remember a time when Jessica Olden hadn't been in his life. Neither could he reconcile the hatred he had felt for her at first. It wasn't her fault that she couldn't take his case, and it wasn't her fault he'd lost custody. The fault was with himself... and the vicious woman he'd married. God, how the hell did DJ stand a chance?

He went back into his daughter's room. DJ was sleeping now, and Dorcas sat by her side. She looked up now, and he was surprised to see regret in her eyes. "I'm sorry, Teddy. I just get so... I'm sorry I was rude to Jessica."

Teddy swallowed back the snort of laughter. Dorcas? Sorry? *Right.* But he had to give it to her. If this was an act, then she was playing the role perfectly. "It's fine." He sat on DJ's other side and swept a hand again onto his sleeping daughter's forehead.

Dorcas was holding DJ's hand. "She's so much more at peace when we three are together."

Teddy didn't respond, not wanting to get into a scene. Instead, he sat back and studied Dorcas. "I'd like DJ for more than a few hours. I want a weekend or two a month. Some time so we can go away, up to Tahoe, or someplace where we can go hiking or cycling for a few days."

He waited for Dorcas to flat out deny him but instead she looked up at him. "Fine."

Was it really going to be this easy? What was she playing at? He asked her just that, and she shrugged. "This is the second time I've nearly lost my daughter, Teddy. Life is too short to hold onto petty animus."

Now he did laugh, shaking his head. "What's your game, Dorcas? Because this whole new Earth Mother thing isn't you. I know you, remember?"

Dorcas's eyes were soft on his. "Maybe not as well as you thought. I'm sorry I kept her from you, Teddy. It was beneath me."

Teddy nodded but said nothing. Dorcas would have to prove she meant what she said—he knew her too well.

Teddy called Jess later that morning to tell her he was staying at the hospital. "Dorcas suggested it."

"She did? Huh." Jess couldn't help the cynical tone in her voice, and she heard Teddy's low chuckle.

"Well, yeah. But gift horse and all that, I get to spend the entire day with my kid for once."

"I'm glad, baby. Call me if you need anything."

"Thank you, beautiful. I'll see you later."

Jess ended the call, smiling. God, she didn't know how parents did it; she would be a nervous wreck the whole time if she had a kid. And DJ sounded like such a great girl, and Jess admitted to herself that she would love to get to know her.

Jeez, Olden, broody much? The thought reminded her that she hadn't checked in with Coco lately, and as she made herself some coffee, she picked up the phone. Coco's phone however went straight to voicemail.

Instead she called India but was surprised to hear her friend sound downbeat. "What's up, boo?"

"It's Massi," her friend confided. "He's... going through some stuff."

"What stuff?"

India sighed. "God, Jess, I feel so guilty. He's been having terrible nightmares, and he's so stressed that everything triggers him. I'm trying to persuade him to see a therapist, but he keeps saying it wasn't him who got abducted and stabbed." Her voice quivered. "We've been arguing."

That shocked Jess. As far as she knew, India and Massi had rarely ever had a cross word between them. "Oh, sweetie."

She heard India pull in a deep breath. "I don't know what to say to him to make him feel better. He keeps saying he should have protected me better, but he... God, Jess, why is this still so painful?"

"Indy... do you understand the magnitude of what happened to you? You were almost killed. We all, all of us who love you, it's like we died, too. Massi... man, he loves you so much that if anything happened to you, it would literally kill him. Of course, there's going to be kickback. I'm surprised it hasn't happened sooner." Jess slowed down, aware her voice was rising. "Sorry."

"You're angry at me, too." India didn't say it as if she were self-pitying herself, more as a statement.

Jess steeled herself. "Yes. A little. Not as much as I was

when I saw you covered in blood and dying. But yes. I'm mad you put yourself in danger, and I know that's unfair."

"No, it's not." India actually sounded more cheerful. "I want someone to get mad at me and yell. I was so damn stupid. Please, Jess, of all of my friends, you're the least likely to bullshit. Yell at me, call me names, get mad. Please?"

"You want me to?" Jess took a deep breath. "India Blue. Do you know how crippling stupid you were? How selfish? Sun had just been shot and you ran away. You ran away from all of us and put yourself into the hands of both a man who rejected you and a man you knew full well wanted to kill you."

"I know. More."

"It was so downright dumb that I'm surprised there's a brain left in your head because, God, India, what the fuck were you thinking?"

"More."

"India... stupid doesn't even cover it. Moronic. Idiotic. You absolute fucking... gah!" Jess let out a yell of long-suppressed frustration, and she heard a strange noise at the end of the line. "India, are you crying?"

But Indy was laughing. "God, I needed to hear that, Jessie. So much. Everyone's been tiptoeing around, but I was a fucking idiot. Suicidal and so damn selfish. How could I have left Sun in that condition? Massi? Jesus, what a dinkus."

Jess started to laugh then, too. "But, God, I love you. I'm so happy you made it, babe."

"Don't be nice or I will cry."

"Alright, doofus."

"Cow."

"Bish."

India laughed. "Couldn't bring yourself to say bitch, could you?"

"Nah. Not you. Never you. Feel better?"

"I do, thank you. Now, I just need to get through to Massi. He'll be leaving for LA in two weeks to start the film with Teddy, and I've got so much work to do here, I can't come with him. I'm worried."

"Indy, look, he'll have me, Coco, Alex... and he and Teddy really hit it off. I can talk to Teddy about keeping an eye on him."

"Would you? But don't make it like he's babysitting; Massi will see through that in a second."

Jess smiled. "Don't worry. Teddy's smoother than that."

"You really like him, don't you?"

Jess was silent for a moment, and India seemed to sense her reticence. "Jess?"

"I do. I like him a lot, Indy, and this is... a new feeling for me. It's a little scary."

India was quiet herself then. "You love him."

Jess swallowed, but she couldn't lie to her best friend. "I do. I'm crazy go nuts for him, Indy, and it scares the shit out of me."

India gave a soft chuckle. "I know that feeling, Jessie. I felt the same way about Massi, from the first night I met him. It is scary, but I think if something is worth it, it should be a little frightening, right? Teddy's lovely."

JESS SAID goodbye to her friend and went out onto the deck to have her coffee and think about her day. It was Saturday, and she had planned to spend it with Teddy. So, now, the day stretched ahead of her, and it was nice not to have anything planned.

SHE DIDN'T NOTICE the man walking on the beach alongside her condo. Taran Googe had borrowed a friend's dog and was walking him as an excuse to skirt Jessica Olden's condo. He could see her now, sitting out on her deck, looking relaxed.

Looking damn beautiful. His cock twitched as he gazed at her from beneath his baseball cap. Beautiful but a fucking ball-busting *bitch*. He'd been humiliated at that party, and he would make her pay for that. Keying her car had been stupid, and he'd half expected the police to come to his apartment last night.

But nothing. It irked him somewhat; to Jessica Olden, he was just a petty annoyance. But not for much longer. Jess Olden would soon learn not to cross Taran Googe. He was going to destroy her life one way or another.

Enjoy your peace, you bitch. The shit's about to hit the fan.

. . .

Teddy kissed DJ's forehead. "I'll come back later, sweetie. Any requests?"

"Twizzlers?" She looked hopefully at him and then Dorcas, who rolled her eyes, but nodded.

"Consider it done." He smiled at his daughter, then nodded at his ex-wife. "I'll come back and relieve you this evening."

"We'll be waiting." Dorcas smiled at him and just for a second, he saw the woman he had fallen in love with all those years ago, before the stardom, before the diva-hood, before the drugs. When she had loved him. He felt a pang of sadness at the way things had ended.

"See you later."

He walked out into the hospital corridor, thanking the nurses he saw standing at the station. He signed a couple of autographs—they had been remarkable in keeping fans away and he could tell they had been dying to ask—and thanked them again. An autograph was the very least he could do.

He headed down to reception, ducking around a pack of *paps* waiting for him with a practiced stealth. As he headed to the main door, he stopped, recognizing a tall man standing, staring out of the window.

"Alex?"

Alex turned to him, but there was such a dead look in his eyes that Teddy almost recoiled. "Jesus, man, what's the matter?" He put his hand on Alex's arm, but the other man simply blinked, as if he didn't recognize him.

"She's gone."

"What? Who's gone?"

Alex's eyes were full of pain and his face cracked as he broke down. "Coco. She was having pain, so I brought her to the emergency room. They said something about, God, I don't know… but she's gone. Our baby… both of them… they're dead."

14

CHAPTER FOURTEEN – SONG TO THE SIREN

Los Angeles

FOR A WARM SPRING DAY, Jess felt chilled to the bone as she watched Coco's casket being lowered into the ground. Around her, people were sobbing, but Coco's closest friends—Alex, India, Massimo, and Sun and Tae who had flown over from Korea—stood as if they were statues. Shell-shocked. Devastated. Jess caught India's eyes, and her friend just shook her head.

None of them could believe this day. Jess felt Teddy squeeze her hand, and she leaned against him gratefully.

The wake was held at Alex and Coco's condo, but Alex was in no fit state to receive guests. The man had lost his best friend and his child to an out-of-the-blue brain hemorrhage. There had been no signs until Coco complained of a crippling headache. She had been even joking around on the car ride over to the hospital.

Jess and India had stepped up to protect Alex at the wake and to make sure the guests were well-tended. There were a lot of Hollywood stars there, but no one was grandstanding or performing. Coco had been well-liked—no, Jess thought, screw that—Coco had been loved in this town. She got the job done and did it with grace and style and warmth, and people loved her.

How could she be gone? How was that possible?

As the guests began to drift away later in the day, Jess went to the guest room to get some air and give herself time to breathe. Teddy followed her, shutting the door behind him and wrapping his arms around her. "You did good, Jessie."

She leaned against him. "I'm not doing so well, baby."

"I know. I doubt there's anything I could say to make you feel better right now, but you did Coco proud today. You and Indy and Massi, and those way-too-pretty Korean boys."

Jess half-smiled. Teddy had been seduced by Sun and Tae, their natural charm shining even through their sadness. "They're sweet boys."

Teddy kissed her temple. "Baby... you know you can let go with me, right? Scream, rant, cry... you haven't cried yet."

"Because I still don't believe it. I just don't." Jess closed her eyes. "I ought to get back."

"Give yourself a few minutes. Indy's looking after Alex, Massi's handling the remainder of the guests."

Jess leaned into him, but then her phone bleeped. "Jesus, not now..." But she checked it. "Fuck. *Fuck.* Are you *shitting* me?" She gaped at her phone, and Teddy gently took it from her. She looked at him as he read the test message from her assistant. "Really, *today*?"

Teddy shook his head, and Jess took her phone back and called Bee.

Her assistant sounded as if she were in tears. "I'm so sorry to call you, Jess, but I thought you should find out from me."

"Is the video online yet?"

"Yes, it went up a few minutes ago."

"Send me the link."

In a few minutes, Jess had cued up the video, and she and Teddy watched it together. The title alone made her want to scream.

Surrounded by death... is Jessica Olden a deadly curse to everyone around her?

Taran Googe's shiny, waxy face stared back at her as he detailed the deaths of Coco, Jess's sister Katie, and the near murder of India, linking each to Jess in the most repellent, nonsensical way. But then, Jess knew, Googe knew this was bullshit. This whole thing was to hurt her, to get revenge for embarrassing him, and he didn't care that it was all provably untrue. It was enough to make her feel like crap, and that's exactly why he had done it today, the day of Coco's funeral.

"Asshole! Fucker!" Jess screamed now at the top of her voice, bringing her friends to the room. As Jess ranted, Teddy filled them in on Googe's video.

"That motherfucker," Alex growled, his grief making him wild with fury for his friend. "I'll beat the living shit out of him."

Sun put his hand on Alex's arm, calming him. "My friend, it's what he wants. He's a bug on a windshield. Jess, is this the moron you told us about?"

Jess nodded. She was watching the video again, and they listened as Taran Googe described the circumstances of her sister's death.

"It must hurt that Jessica's own father blames her for Katie's suicide. If Jess had just paid more attention to her, been less selfish... it's hard to hear the grief in the man's voice." Taran's voice was soft; he was acting as if he too felt the pain of Katie's death.

Jess had run out of expletives, and now she felt hot tears in her eyes. "How dare he? How *dare* he use Katie? Use Coco to hurt me? Bastard. He needs to get their names out of his filthy, disgusting mouth."

Teddy gently took her phone. "We will deal with Googe, my love. We will. For now, though... none of what he says will be taken seriously. He wanted to hit you at your most vulnerable, and," and he smiled gently, "he knows those times when Jess Olden is vulnerable are very few and far between. He timed this purposefully."

"He did," India said now, taking Jess's hand in his. "Everyone who loves you, everyone who cares, knows this is crap. It can't hurt you, not really."

Jess nodded but now she felt numb. Everyone in this room had had to deal with loss, with grief. Nobody was immune, not even her.

TEDDY TOOK HER HOME LATER, but she insisted he go see DJ rather than sit with her. "Don't waste a moment with her," she urged, and Teddy kissed her.

"I'll be back tonight."

"I'll wait up."

When he got back to the hospital, DJ was asleep. Dorcas looked pale and tired. "How was the funeral?"

"Painful. How's the kiddo?"

Dorcas sighed. "She took a little turn for the worse again. They're running more tests, but so far, they've come up with nothing." She studied him. "You look tired."

"So do you. Why don't you go home, get a shower, eat, sleep. I can stay with DJ."

"Wouldn't you rather be with your girlfriend?"

Teddy looked at her sharply. "What does that mean?"

Dorcas looked innocent. "I didn't mean anything by it. It's been a hard day for both of you."

Teddy felt his shoulders slump. "DJ is my first priority."

Dorcas nodded and stood. "Look, I will go get some food and some coffee, but I want to stay with her. She's very sleepy. The stomach cramps were keeping her awake for most of the day, so they gave her something to sleep. I wish they would find something, anything." She turned her face away, and Teddy saw tears glint in her eyes before she hid her face.

He went to her and patted her shoulder, somewhat awkwardly. "She's okay, Dorcas. It'll be nothing more than a bad stomach flu. Come on now, you know this. Go get some food, some rest. If you want to come back, fine, but she's my daughter, too. I can take care of her."

Dorcas nodded, then to his surprise, she kissed his cheek. "You are a good father, Teddy."

She was gone before he could respond, leaving him shocked and a little confused. Was she really that concerned about DJ that her whole personality had changed? Was she finally taking parenting seriously?

He hoped so.

India closed the door of the guest room and went to climb on the bed. "Alex is asleep, finally. I think that half bottle of scotch helped. Sun and Tae are still up, jetlagged." She sighed and looked over at Massimo. "Hey."

"Hey." He held out his arms and she went into them. "You okay?"

"No, but I will be. You?" She searched his eyes, saw the pain deep within them. "It's unbelievable, right?"

He nodded but stayed silent. India kissed him "Talk to me."

"Nothing to say. It just sucks, is all."

India stroked his cheek. "Your Americanisms are improving."

Massimo pressed his lips to hers. "How about I improve my other skills?"

India smiled softly. "Good idea. Make us forget this terrible day." She chuckled softly. "Sorry, that wasn't the most romantic thing I've ever said."

Massimo kissed her again and gently rolled her onto her back. "I think anything goes on a day like this. If you don't want to make love, I understand, you know."

"No, I do," she whispered back to him, "I really do. I need to, you know. I need to feel close to you today of all days." She grinned wryly. "But then again, I always do."

Massimo smiled and for the first time in a while, she saw the fun in his eyes that she so loved. "I love you, India Blue. I know we're not married yet, but I already feel like your husband."

They began to make love, stroking and caressing each other, every touch a balm to their grief, their frayed nerves. They knew each other's bodies so well now, but every cell in India's body was ignited by Massimo, still, after all this time. When he thrust into her, they made love slowly, enjoying each and every sensation, building up to a quiet climax, each muffling the other's cry with their lips. As he came inside of her, India felt his cock pumping thick creamy cum deep into her belly, and she smiled, kissing his lips, his throat, nuzzling her nose against his. "I love you," she murmured and kissed him again.

Afterward, they fell asleep, but she woke in the early morning to find the bed empty.

India padded around the apartment looking for Massimo but couldn't find him anywhere. She went out onto the deck, scanning the beach for him and saw a solitary figure walking along the shore. It wasn't even dawn yet, but the moon was bright and so she climbed down the steps onto the beach and headed towards her lover. As she got close, she could hear him talking to himself, angry, cursing in Italian, and the sudden shock of his rage frightened her. "Massi?"

Massimo froze and took a moment before he turned to her. "Go back to the house, Indy."

"What's wrong?"

"Go back to the house. Please."

There was a tone in his voice she had never heard before and it confused her. He sounded... aggressive. What? Her Massi?

"Massimo..."

"*Go back to the house!*"

India stumbled away from him, stunned, shattered by the way he screamed the words at her, and she turned and ran. By the time she reached the deck, she was trembling so much that she could barely walk, and she climbed the steps on all fours and collapsed to the ground, shaking. She panted for air, looking back to where she could see him, crouching, his head in his hands.

India felt an arm snake around her shoulders. Sun. "I heard... are you okay, Indy?"

She shook her head and let him pick her up and walk her inside. Tae, his hair sticking up in all directions, was inside, his eyes large and confused. "What was that?"

"I think Massimo is… upset." Sun said discreetly, but Indy saw the look that passed between her friends.

"Did I miss something?" Her voice shook, but she wanted to know what they knew, what she didn't know about her lover.

Sun sighed. "Indy, we've been concerned… since we got here. Massimo seems different, stressed."

"Ready to snap," Tae said with a little more force. "Like anything could set him off." He sat down next to India and took her hand. "Have you noticed anything?"

India nodded, feeling numb. "Yes. A few times but when I try to address it, he just… I don't get it. We made love tonight, and everything seemed okay, under the circumstances." She looked out of the window. "He's never, ever shouted at me like that. *Never.*"

As she spoke, a shadow passed across the light in the room and Massimo pushed open the glass door. He stepped into the room, not looking at any of them in the eye. "Fellas… can we have a moment?"

Tae nodded, but Sun looked at India, his eyes questioning. She nodded at him, and he squeezed her hand, then he and Tae went back to their own room. Massimo came and sat down opposite her, but didn't attempt to touch her. "I'm sorry."

India nodded but didn't speak. He would not meet her eye.

Massimo rubbed his face. "I think... I think I might need..."

"To see someone?"

He met her gaze then. "I might need some... space."

Every cell in her body shrieked with pain. "Space? From... me?"

Massimo nodded, and India's heart shattered into a billion pieces. But she took a deep breath in. "If that's what you need."

Massimo stood up. "I'll call a cab."

God, the pain, the shock of it. "Right now?"

He nodded, looking away from her. "Yes."

India stood frozen as he went to their room. In a few moments, he was back with his bag. "I'm sorry," he said again, then he did meet her eyes. "I love you."

"But it's not enough, is it?"

Massimo hesitated, then nodded. "No, it's not. Not right now."

India felt like a white-hot spike had been driven through her chest. She would take Braydon Carter's knife over and over again rather than this. She watched as her love, *the* love of her life, walked out of the beach house, heard him get into the cab and drive away, and felt like she couldn't move, couldn't breathe.

Eventually, she felt Sun's arms around her, and he took her back to his and Tae's room, where they both held her for the rest of the night.

CHAPTER FIFTEEN – WHAT KIND OF MAN?

Los Angeles

JESS BURIED herself in her work, wanting to forget the pain of Coco's death, the sadness over India and Massimo's break-up. She could barely believe it. Instead, she focused on taking down Taran Googe. He'd crossed a line when he'd brought Coco and Katie into it, and she wanted to destroy the asshole before he could do any harm.

So intent on revenge was she that she didn't noticed the concern on her friends' and colleagues' faces. In the end, Bee, her assistant, called Teddy, nervous and edgy and asked him to help. "I'm so sorry to intrude like this but we're so worried."

"It's okay," Teddy told her, "I appreciate you coming to

me. You always can when it's to do with Jess, alright? Know that."

"Thank you, Mr. Hood."

"It's Teddy, Bee, honestly."

"Thank you, Teddy."

JESS WAS STILL WORKING when Teddy came home from the hospital with news of DJ. "She's been released," he beamed at Jess, who smiled, nodding in her relief.

"Do they know yet what it was?"

"They think a virus that may have reoccurred, but they're not one hundred percent. She seems fine now though." He sat down on the couch next to her, hooking his arm around her shoulders and kissing her cheek. "You smell so good."

"I just had a soak in the tub." She rolled her shoulders, and Teddy could see the tension rolling off of her. He glanced at her computer screen and sighed. Taran Googe. Gently, he took the laptop from her and closed it. "Enough."

For a moment he thought she might argue with him but then she nodded and let him wrap his arms around her. "Going after that little pissant isn't going to bring Coco back."

"I know." Jess pressed her lips to his. "I'm sorry you got dragged into all of this."

"Hey, I dragged you into my shit right from the start."

"That's different; you paid me to deal with your shit."

But she smiled softly at him. "But I would have done it for free, gladly."

"Good, because damn, you is *expensive*, girl." He grinned at her, and she laughed, a sound he had missed over the last couple of weeks.

"I'll take my fee in sex," she nodded, her eyes wide and innocent and he laughed.

"Now you're talking." He kissed her again and felt her press her body to his. They both groaned when her phone buzzed. "Leave it."

"I can't. Technically it could be a client."

He sighed but let her pick up the phone. He got up, signaling to her that he was going to get a drink and asking her if she wanted one. Jess nodded and answered her call.

Teddy went into the kitchen and snagged a couple of beers from the fridge. As he closed it, he saw a photograph stuck to the door with a magnet. It was Jess, India, and Coco, laughing together, happy, joyous. It had to be a few years old, they all looked younger and more carefree—except India, who still had a haunted look in her eyes, unsurprising with what she had been going through at the time, being stalked by an obsessive man.

Teddy chewed his lip. Was Jess being too obsessive about revenge on Googe? He didn't want to think so, but he knew she was focusing her grief on the man. Teddy was uneasy about it. Maybe he should pay Googe a visit himself, ask him to back off.

He heard Jess's voice raise and went back into the living

room. She was just ending the call, but she looked annoyed. "What is it?"

Jess looked up at him. "It's Dorcas."

His heart sank. "What now?"

Jess hesitated. "Teddy... she called Child Protective Services. She's asking for an investigation into why DJ got sick right after she visited with you. She's saying she thinks you have something to do with DJ getting sick."

AFTER THE UPSET came the anger. *You want space, here, take it, Massimo. How does half a world away suit you?* India asked Sun and Tae if she could fly back to Seoul with them, and they agreed... eventually. Both of them had told her they thought it would be best to stay for Massimo, but she was angry at him, hurt beyond all measure, and they could not persuade her to stay.

Alex, still consumed by grief, had made plans to go back stay with his parents for a while. Jess had Teddy, and so as India boarded the plane to Korea, she had no regrets. She was so angry with Massimo, and she knew it was unreasonable, given what she had put him through, but why not work it out together?

She had called his mother in Italy, but Giovanna had told her that her eldest child hadn't come home. "If he does, you'll be the first to know, *piccolo*," his mother had promised India, her voice warm, and India knew she would keep her word. Their relationship hadn't started out well, but over the period of India's recovery, they had grown extremely close.

So India didn't know where Massimo had gone, but when he was spotted by paparazzi in Rome, her imagination ran wild. She called his ex-girlfriend, Valentina, who assured her he was not with her. "I have moved on, dear one, and so has Massimo. If, and it's a big if, *if* I see him, I will let you know."

But India didn't trust the woman, and when she called Massimo's younger siblings Grazia and Francesco, film students in the Italian capital, they told they had not seen him either. "We just don't know, Indy," Grazia said, sounded tearful. "He's never done this before."

I drove him to it. India leaned her head against the plane window and felt like crying. They were over the Pacific Ocean now with night falling. Next to her, Sun and Tae were asleep, adorable, leaning on each other, their fingers laced together even as they slept. Sun's slightly chubby cheeks were resting on Tae's shoulder. It eased her heart to see them so happy together, but it made her heart pound with loneliness, too.

She kept reliving the night of her abduction, or rather, the night she had run from Seoul, from Massimo, from the critically injured Sun. That had been the moment she had lost Massimo. Fuck. She'd nearly lost her life, and now she had lost her love.

And she was running away… again. India closed her eyes. What a fucking mess. She rummaged in her bag and took out of bottle of Ambien, throwing one back with some soda. If she couldn't work things out, she'd rather just sleep.

IT TOOK everything Jess had in her to persuade Teddy not to go straight to Dorcas's home and demanded to know what the hell she was up to. "What have you just told me about Googe, Teddy? Don't engage. Don't fight. Knowing Dorcas, this is just another ploy. You haven't done anything wrong, so there's no need to worry about this. It's just a power play."

"A power play that says I've been abusing my daughter!" Teddy was apoplectic.

Jess shook her head, her hands on his shoulders. "No. No one believes it. No one. Dorcas will play it like she's just covering her bases. Trust me, in the next few days, when CPS has interviewed you and found no wrongdoing, she'll be in the press telling them of course she knew you hadn't done anything wrong. She'll even be 'wounded' that it was even suggested. She'll defend you to the hilt."

Teddy gazed at her, his anger cooling. "You think?"

"I know. I've dealt with narcissists like Dorcas many, many times before. And believe me, while this is bad, it doesn't even compare to some of the games I've seen." Jess felt confident enough to drop her hands from his shoulders. "Baby, I know it's frustrating, but we've seen the press. No one is buying that you hurt DJ—no one. Let her blow herself out; if she continues along with this narrative, the press and the public will turn against her."

Teddy's shoulders relaxed. "You think?"

"I *know*. Dorcas isn't that bright, but she's not stupid. She's lost the publicity battle since your split and she knows it. So, she's trying to reframe herself as the single mother whose only focus is her child. But she knows your popularity has never been higher. Teddy, people were relieved when you split. *Relieved.* What does that tell you?" Jess smiled at him. "I get the impression that most of your friends in this business couldn't stand that you were ever together."

"Yeah," Teddy nodded, giving a soft chuckle. "I'm getting that impression, too." He smiled at her gratefully. "Thanks, beautiful. I needed to hear all of that."

"Hey, we're a team. You talk me down, I talk you down." Jess sighed suddenly, and Teddy knew she was thinking about India and Massimo.

"Hey, you can't solve everyone's problems, baby."

"I know. God, what a shitty couple of years." She looked up at him. "You might be the best thing that's happened to me."

"I hope so. I'll try to be." He took her in his arms. "I'm crazy about you, Ms. Olden."

"Right back at you, Mr. Movie Star."

Teddy laughed. "Ha. I'm still that good old boy from Nowheresville."

Jess smiled up at him, her dark eyes shining. "You're *my* good old boy."

"Damn straight." He touched his lips to hers gently,

then with more urgency. He nuzzled his nose against hers. "You busy right now?"

He felt her mouth curve up in a grin. "Right now?"

Teddy slid his hand between her legs and began to rub. "*Right* now..."

Jess gave a moan of desire. "You're a bad influence..."

He swept her up into his arms and carried her to the bedroom, dropping her onto the bed and covering her body with his own. "You're a talented, beautiful, powerful woman, Jessica Olden. If life was fair, you'd be the one feted by Hollywood, by the entire world."

"Sweet talker. Now shut up and fuck me," she said with a wide grin and he laughed.

"And you're a lunatic. My lunatic."

"Damn straight."

There was no more talking then as they kissed, frantically pulling each other's clothes off until they lay naked, skin-on-skin, and Teddy was hitching her legs around his waist. He kissed her as his rock-hard cock thrust deep inside her and heard her moan of pleasure. They made love hard and fast, clawing and tearing at each other, a kind of urgency to their lovemaking.

He watched her as she came, her lovely face flushing a deep pink, her eyes closing, her head flung back and thought he had never seen a more beautiful sight.

Neither of them saw Taran Googe watching them through the bedroom window. Had they been at Teddy's place, he wouldn't have gotten near to the house but here at the relatively open neighborhood where Jess lived, it was easy.

Googe couldn't take his eyes of Jess Olden's gloriously naked body. Christ, she was sensational... no wonder Teddy Hood had fallen for her. He wondered how the public would feel about Hood fucking his lawyer... would they care? Probably not. They'd only have to think about how gorgeous Jess was to automatically make that assumption, anyway. Everybody fucked everybody else in this town.

He watched her now, laughing and joking around with Hood, then as Hood went down on her, Googe's eyes were glued to her breasts, full, ripe, undulating with the rhythm of their lovemaking. He wanted to fuck her and hurt her at the same time.

Jesus. How had that thought occurred to him? Googe was a troublemaker, an instigator, but he wasn't violent. He turned away from the window and climbed back down onto the sidewalk. He'd never hurt anyone in his life, but as he walked down the block towards his car, he realized that his anger towards Jess Olden was more than just annoyance.

Boy. The way she had spat the word at him, the humiliation of it... Jesus. Physical emasculation would have been less painful. He'd wanted to kill her right then and there, in front of all those asshole party guests who were laughing at him.

Kill. Jesus, calm down. Taran shook his head as he got

into his car. No, he wasn't that guy. He'd get his revenge by humiliating her, by losing her business and reputation. He wasn't going to do anything to Jess Olden that would require him going to jail. He wasn't dumb, and more than that, he could never harm anyone, not even that bitch.

He wasn't *that* guy. Was he?

16

CHAPTER SIXTEEN – SO FAR AWAY

Seoul, South Korea

INDIA HAD BEEN in Seoul for two weeks, and she'd heard nothing from Massimo. She called him every night on his cell phone but never left a message. She could tell Sun and Tae were worried about her, but she couldn't help but be miserable.

She apologized to them over and over for intruding again on their lives. "I'm doing it again, aren't I? You and Sun need your space." She said this to Tae one afternoon when Sun had been called away and there was just the two of them in the apartment. "I'm sorry, Tae, I should never have come."

"Sweetheart, it's okay. You needed us." Tae stroked her hair. "We're family. This will get better, I promise."

"Why did he leave?"

"Why did you?"

One of the things she loved about Tae was that he didn't soft-soap things. He said this without rancor or judgement, just as a way of trying to make her think.

"I've been thinking it over. The shock of Sun's shooting... I thought I was a jinx. I thought that if..." She stopped and looked at Tae guiltily. "If I was out of the way, you all could be happy. That the hurt would stop."

Tae took her hand. "And Massimo? He is hurting, too. Coco's death just brought back the fact that he nearly lost you. He's been on the edge since the day you were brought to the hospital. He was going to break some time."

India chewed this over. "He's been talking to you?"

Tae smiled at her kindly. "We both nearly lost someone. We had things in common, and so, when Massi didn't want to burden you while you were recovering, we leaned on each other."

"But I'm better now. Why didn't he come to me? I'm not a baby."

"You're not better. You just think you are. Do you think none of us can't see the pain you're in? Not just the physical pain, but the rock back from killing a man?"

"I would do it all over again," she said vehemently, riled up now. "I don't regret for one moment killing Carter. For Sun, for my mom, for myself. Not one minute."

Tae put his arm around her. "And you shouldn't. I'm

not talking about Carter himself, per se, but anyone would be affected by killing. It shows you're human, and whether you acknowledge it or not, it's affected you, changed you."

"This isn't about me, this is about Massimo."

"It's about both of you. Give him time."

SUN ARRIVED back a couple of hours later, a guilty look in his eyes, and he and Tae disappeared into their bedroom. India could hear them talking in Korean—she spoke a little herself but couldn't make out what they were arguing about. When she heard the door to the apartment slam, she went out to see Sun staring unhappily at the door.

"Sunbeam? You okay?"

Sun blinked as if he'd forgotten she was there. He looked at her and pulled a face. "Tae is pissed at me. I did something. Don't worry, he'll be back soon."

"What did you do?"

"Nothing serious, but he thinks I'm interfering with... something."

"What?" India had never seen him look so guilty, and yet there was excitement in his eyes.

"Just something."

AN HOUR LATER, India found out exactly what Sun had done when Tae returned. Tae came in first, then looked at her. "Indy..."

Behind him, Massimo walked into the apartment. He

looked terrible, his eyes shadowed by violet circles, his face unshaven. "India."

India stood, glancing at Sun uncertainly. "This is what you did?"

Sun nodded. "I found him, had him brought to Seoul. You'll never guess where he was."

"Where?"

"Busan. He might have wanted his space but obviously not that much." His tone was amused. "Luckily for me, a friend of a friend down there called me."

Both Tae and Massimo rolled their eyes but India wasn't impressed with any of them. "Sun... Tae..."

They took the hint and left them alone. She gazed at Massimo. His eyes were soft, apologetic... broken. But she wasn't letting him off the hook that easily. "Never again," she said. "You never again get to throw my mistake back in my face."

"I know."

"You should have told me how much pain you were in."

"Ditto," he said gently and smiled.

"Don't."

"Sorry." He came closer, looking gratified when she didn't back away. "I am sorry, Indy. Sorry for shouting at you, sorry for leaving. It was dumb."

India couldn't think of anything to say, so for a moment, she just stared at him. Then, surprising both of them, she opened her arms, and he went into them. They held each other tightly for a long time before either spoke again.

"I need help," he murmured eventually, and she nodded.

"I know. We'll go home and get you what you need." She cradled his face in her hands. "You look terrible."

"I know. Sure you want this old man?"

India smiled up at him. "Always. Just don't run away again, and I promise you, right here, neither will I."

"Deal." He kissed her, and she wound her fingers in his dark hair and kissed him back, grateful to her friends for helping her out again.

SUN AND TAE drove them to the airport the next day, and India and Massimo thanked their friends for again being there for them. "The next time we see you, we'll be getting married." Sun grinned at them. "I can't wait."

LOS ANGELES

TARAN GOOGE HAD UPLOADED another video slamming Jess, but she chose this time to ignore it. She was more focused on getting Teddy through his CPS interview. "The fact it's just an interview tells you something. They don't believe anything is wrong either."

To their surprise, Dorcas hadn't attempted to change the visitation to DJ, but as Jess had predicted, she had played the rest of it out as expected. She was 'bemused' by the CPS investigation. "Teddy is a wonderful father," she said with a smile at a press conference for her latest movie. "Wonderful, loving, supportive. We are lucky to have him in our lives." Looking right down the camera, she smiled. "We are both so lucky to have a man like Teddy in our lives."

"Bleurgh." Jess made a gagging noise as they watched the interview in her office, and Teddy grinned.

"That's why she's an actress."

Jess half-smiled, but then fixed him with a steady gaze. "She wants you back."

"Nope."

"Yes, she does, and you know it, too. That's what the whole..." She trailed off as something occurred to her and Teddy raised his eyebrows.

"What?"

Jess swallowed hard. "No, nothing. But she does want you back." She gave him a watery smile, disturbed by her thoughts, but she didn't want to say them out loud, at least not for now. The thought, the idea of a mother... no. Don't even think it. "Who wouldn't want you?" She grinned at Teddy now, determined to distract him and it worked.

"Well, I know," he posed for her, "I'm a dreamboat."

Later, when Teddy had fallen asleep, Jess slipped from the bed and went to her office, closing the door behind her. She fired up her laptop and browsed the internet, trying to find out more about her theory. Her horrifying theory. She desperately didn't want it to be true, but... Would Dorcas Prettyman harm her daughter to get Teddy back?

Her gut instinct told her yes, and it made her feel sick to her stomach. Jess lost track of time as she scrolled through various web pages, learning the name of the condition by heart: Munchausen's by proxy.

Jess closed her eyes. She knew from experience how insidious a parent's abuse could be, how a person's apparent charm and softness could hide a myriad of evil acts. Her father, for instance. His amiability shielded him from the judgement of others; if they had only known what he did to his daughters. The aggressive behaviour, the shouting, the emotional abuse.

The sexual abuse. Jess had been the lucky one. He hadn't started that until Jess had left the house. Katie had been his target, and Jess had never known until after Katie had died. Jess had received a letter from her sister a day after Katie's death, and it had destroyed her. Katie had detailed everything he had done to her. Jess took the letter to the police, but her father's influence was wide, and the letter, and any investigation, disappeared.

Jess never went home again. She changed majors from art to law and never looked back. So, now, her *spidey* senses were heightened, and they were tingling now. Dorcas Prettyman was capable of the worst; she knew it and she was going to expose her.

Jess went back to bed then, and in the morning, not giving anything away, she told Teddy that she would like to meet DJ.

CHAPTER SEVENTEEN – WHEREVER I GO

Los Angeles

THE CPS INTERVIEW went as well as it could. The investigators were even a little apologetic for calling Teddy in, and after he and Jess left, he felt his whole body relax. He took Jess's hand. "Thanks for getting me through that, baby."

Jess grinned at him. "I didn't do anything, honey bunch. They knew it was bull crap before they even called the meeting, but legally, they have to investigate. I see Dorcas still has some legal people on her side."

Teddy laughed. He couldn't be pissed on a day like this. Later, he would pick DJ up, then he would take her to meet Jess at a local park. Jess was nervous, he could tell, but he had been delighted when she had told him she wanted to meet DJ. Her sweet face was creased with worry as she told him that, as if he'd object, but the truth was, he had been yearning for his two favorite people to meet.

"Listen, I have to meet my agent for lunch. Want to join?"

Jess smiled. "No, I won't, thanks. I've a ton of work at the office, and I've been neglecting it. But I can't wait for later. When are you picking DJ up?"

"Three. We'll be at the park by three thirty."

"Then I'll see you there."

JESS WAVED Teddy off as he drove away from the CPS office, then took a cab back to her own office. As she stepped out, she noticed her team all gathered on the sidewalk. Frowning, she went over to them. "What's going on?"

"There was an envelope delivered, addressed to you. Bee opened it, and all that there was inside was white powder."

Jess's heart sank. No way... "Where is she?"

"Still inside. They've shut the offices down. They think it's a fake substance, but they have to be sure. We were at lunch which is why we're not being quarantined. Bee called us and told us to stay away."

Jess sighed, looking up at the building. "Well... look. If the police have cleared you to go home, do that. Don't worry, you'll still be paid, but we obviously won't be able to work until we're cleared."

She spoke to the detective who came to see them, and

he agreed with her. When her staff had left, she asked after Bee. She hadn't wanted to in front of her staff in case the news was bad.

The detective reassured her. "She's fine. We have to work on the assumption that the substance is aggressive, but at the moment, there is no indication that it is insidious. Your colleague is fine, being assessed by doctors from HASMAT. Obviously we can't let you inside, but if you like, you can call her."

Jess thanked him and did just that. "Hey, Bee, it's me. Can you talk?"

"I can, boss, don't worry, I'm fine. It was just a little shocking, but they don't seem to be overly alarmed. They think it's just chalk or talc or something but until the tests come back..."

"I'm so sorry, Bee. Was there any identifying marks on the envelope?"

"No, it was hand-delivered. Thing is, no one saw by whom."

"What about the security cameras?"

"They're looking into that now."

Jess sighed. "Well, the police will want to know. I'm just trying to think of someone I've pissed off that much."

Bee snorted. "I don't think we have to look too far. I've already told the police about Googe."

"Well, we have to be careful, Bee. We have to be absolutely sure."

"I know, but at the very least, they'll have to interview

the a-hole. If that doesn't scare him into leaving you the hell alone, I don't know what will. And it *is* him."

Jess chuckled at Bee's disgruntled tone. "Oh, Bumble Bee, I do love you. Remind me to give you a huge pay hike after this."

"Ha, I've recorded you saying that, and this counts as informing you, so don't even think of taking me to court."

Jess laughed. "You are a nut job. Remind me to fire you."

"Uh-uh, too late. I turned off the recorder."

JESS WAITED AROUND for any news, but eventually, the detective in charge told her to go home. "There really is nothing for you to do, Miss Olden. We'll be in touch."

Her phone rang as she was walking back to her car, and she suddenly realized she was already running late for Teddy and DJ. Teddy sounded worried. "Are you okay?"

She told him what had happened. "Jesus, Jessie... is this Googe?"

"Can't think of anyone else who would stoop so low. Look, don't worry, the responders seem to think it's a hoax, and Bee assures me she is fine. Listen, I'm in the car now and on my way to you."

"You sure?"

"Of course, I've been looking forward to seeing DJ all day."

His voice was tender as he replied, and she could tell he was touched. "We'll be waiting."

. . .

Jess had brought some clothes to change into after work, so she ducked into a gas station and changed quickly on the way to the park. She went into the store and bought some snacks and some sodas, and then returned to her car.

There was a faint prickling on the back of her neck suddenly and the sense of being watched. She glanced around but couldn't see anyone suspicious. Paranoia won't help matters, but as she pulled the car back onto the highway, she couldn't help glancing in her rearview mirror for any cars that might be following her.

She'd almost talked herself into a panic by the time she reached the park, but as soon as she saw Teddy and DJ playing with a ball, her body relaxed. *No one is following you, woman.* She watched them play for a few minutes before getting out. She'd tied her hair back and worn a t-shirt and jeans to look less formidable than her everyday work lawyer gear.

Teddy looked up and saw her as she approached and waved, his face lighting up, which make her heart swell with love. God, he was handsome... her eyes flicked to the young girl beside him and again, her chest hurt. DJ was the image of her father, dark hair, messy and long, and bright blue eyes. DJ smiled shyly at Jess as she approached, and after kissing Teddy's cheek, Jess crouched down to DJ's height. "Hey, there. It's great to meet you at last, DJ."

She grinned as DJ held out a tiny hand for her to

shake, and she shook it, nodding. "Hello, Jess. Daddy really likes you."

Teddy rolled his eyes, grinning as they both laughed at him. "I have no game."

"Nope." Jess smiled at DJ. "Listen, I don't know about you both, but I skipped lunch. Want to go grab something to eat?"

DJ nodded eagerly, and Teddy nodded. "There's a burger and shake joint a couple of blocks from here. Shall we walk?"

IF TEDDY THOUGHT DJ would be shy around Jess, he had a surprise coming. DJ took to Jess from the start and even held her hand as they walked to the burger place. She sat next to Jess as they ordered, chatting happily then when their food came, they all fell on the burgers like starving animals.

Teddy barely had to run interference at all, so easily did Jess and DJ chat with each other. Only when Jess had to take a call did she step away from them for a moment, and Teddy smiled at his daughter. "Well?"

DJ's eye were shining. "I like her a lot, Dad. She's fun and so pretty."

Teddy grinned. "I had noticed."

"And she's…" DJ faltered, looking for the right word. "I feel easy around her. I don't know if that is the right word."

"Well, what do you mean by it?"

DJ stole a French fry from his plate. "I think I mean... I'm not scared around her."

"You shouldn't be scared around anyone, boo." Teddy frowned. "Who are you scared around? Someone at school?"

DJ shook her head, then her little face went red. "No one, Daddy, I promise. I just mean I like Jessie a lot."

Teddy smoothed his daughter's hair, not convinced by her admission. "You sure? Because if anyone upsets you..."

"No. It's okay, Daddy. Here's Jessie."

Jess had come back to the table, and he could see relief in her eyes. "That was Bee. She's been released. The powder was just alum, so we can go back to work tomorrow. Sorry I interrupted our meal."

Teddy took her hand as she sat back down next to DJ. "It's no problem."

"What's alum?" DJ was pulling her burger apart and removing the tomato. She looked up at them, clearly expecting an answer.

"It's... a kind of chemical, darling."

"Like poison?"

Teddy and Jess exchanged an alarmed look. "No, sweetheart, it's used in cooking and medicine and things."

"Is it in my medicine?"

"Your medicine?"

DJ nodded. "Mommy gives me vitamins in the morning."

Teddy relaxed. "I don't know, darling, but vitamins are

different from medicine, kind of. Medicine is when you're sick, remember?"

"I know. Can we have ice cream after?"

Teddy was relieved the interrogation was over. "Of course, bubba." He smiled at Jess, who seemed preoccupied, chewing her lip, her eyes distant. "Jess?"

She looked up.

"DJ was just telling me that she likes you."

Jess smiled at the young girl. "I'm so glad, DJ. I like you very much, too. I'd like to spend more time with you, if that's okay?"

"Oh, yes..."

"Would you both like to come to my house? It's on the beach... It's not grand, I'm afraid, but at least the ocean is right there."

DJ grinned. "Do you have a dog?"

"I don't, why? Do you like dogs?"

DJ nodded enthusiastically, and Teddy laughed. "Don't go down that rabbit hole, Jess, I beg you. She'll have you at the dog pound before you can say Fido."

"Daddy!" DJ's face was the picture of betrayal.

JESS LAUGHED, drawn to the young girl, and she wasn't someone who bonded easily with kids. But DJ had a worldly air about her—she was intelligent, curious and warm. Just like her father... Jess watched them joking around with each other, and she had the strangest pull in her chest. She'd never had a happy family and never thought she would, but with Teddy and now DJ, there was a hope that maybe it could happen.

Don't trust it. Her natural pessimism was screaming at her that this couldn't last, that she was dreaming, but still, for the rest of the afternoon, she allowed herself to fantasize.

18
CHAPTER EIGHTEEN – NEVER BE THE SAME

Teddy drove DJ back to Dorcas's place, promising to 'be home soon' to Jess. *Wow.* It was true though: her condo had become their base. More than a few of Teddy's clothes had migrated to her closet over the past few months as had his bathing and hygiene products to her bathroom.

Remarkably, having never lived with a man, Jess found she didn't mind his stuff being in her space. It fit. His books alongside hers on the coffee table, a couple of his vinyl records next to her stack near the stereo.

But then again, it was just like Teddy. He fit into her world so well. She was still smiling about it when she turned into her driveway and turned off the ignition.

She knew something was wrong instantly. Even though this was a safe neighborhood, there were a few burglaries—it was a rich part of town, after all—and so everyone had security out the wazoo. She was used to her security camera sensor kicking into action every time she pulled up in the car, but tonight, it didn't move, nor did the light flicker on. For a moment, she sat in the car, trying to see if she noticed anything out of place. The door to her condo was shut, but every light around her place had cut out. She glanced down the street to see if it was neighborhood outage, but further down, she could see other places lit up as dusk fell.

From her bag, she took out her pepper spray and got out of the car. She hadn't studied Krav Maga for so many years to not be able to protect herself. Jess walked towards her door, alert from any attack from behind. Yeah, sometimes paranoia was a good thing... but she reached the door without incident. She grasped the door handle... and recoiled. It was wet with a sticky substance and now she could smell a rust-and-salt smell.

Blood. "Shit..." She opened her door, trying not to touch too much and stepped into her home, flicking on the interior light with her elbow. Her shoe squelched down onto something soft, and she grimaced when she saw what it was. Two or three dead rats had been shoved through her mail slot.

Jess cursed and went to wash her hands. She didn't think it was anything to be concerned about, but given what had happened at her office, she called the detective and reported it anyway.

The detective, Liam Green, told her she was right to call him. "This could be a campaign, and it's better we know everything, that we catalog everything. Someone will be over to take photographs and any finger prints."

Jess thanked him but as she ended the call, she sighed. More intrusion. She left the mess at the door and went to take a shower, hoping to get some of the icky feeling off her skin.

TEDDY HAD JUST SAID goodbye to DJ, spoken briefly with a seemingly friendly Dorcas, and was walking back to the car when he heard someone call his name. He turned to see Johanna behind him. She was glancing nervously behind him, as if afraid Dorcas would see her and scream at her. Teddy felt sorry for the woman—how the hell did she put up with her?

He got his answer as Johanna began to speak. "Mr. Hood, I'm sorry to bother you, and please, know that I'm telling you this not out of—"

"What it is, Johanna?" He didn't interrupt her to be rude, but he could see she was on the edge of tears.

"It's—"

"Johanna? Why are you out here? DJ is getting ready for bed. Go help her, please." Dorcas's tone was sharp but cool.

Johanna turned on her heel, not looking at Teddy again, and Teddy sighed in frustration. He looked at Dorcas. "She was just talking to me, Dorcas. Why did you have to do that? She could have been wanting to talk to me about DJ."

"It wasn't about DJ." Dorcas came closer, her hand on her chest, a sorrowful look in her eyes. "Darling, Johanna is just getting old and she imagines things. She thinks DJ's room is haunted, and that the maid is stealing from her. She won't retire, and DJ is so attached..." She gave a long-suffering sigh. "I swear sometimes, it's like looking after two kids."

Teddy wasn't convinced. "So, she was coming to me because..."

"She wants a raise. I'd give it to her, but as you know, I'm a single mother.

Teddy didn't even to bother to hide his annoyance. "No doubt Johanna would like more than minimum wage for basically doing your job for you." He hadn't meant to snap, but Dorcas's ploy was the same as ever.

"You know, you could be kinder. I'm doing my best. I know I haven't been the greatest mother, but I've changed. If you were around more you would see that, but, whatever."

Dorcas turned away, but not before she let Teddy see the tears in her eyes. Teddy sighed. "Look, Dory, there's nothing to say we can't spend time together as a *family*, but you and I are over. You know this, come on now. I don't say it to hurt you."

"Don't you?"

His eyes softened. "No. I really don't."

Dorcas half-smiled. "It's been a long time since you called me Dory. You always used to, back in the day."

"Back in the day, we were friends as well as lovers. You were Dory then. I'm not saying I haven't changed, too."

Dorcas sighed. "You haven't, not really. Except you got tired of my bullshit, and if I'm being fair, I can't blame you for that. You're still the sweet guy I fell in love with."

Teddy was silent, stopping himself from asking why she had put him through the last year of hell if she thought so. Eventually, he turned to go. "I'm late. I'll see you tomorrow, Dorcas."

"DJ can stay the night with you tomorrow, if you want."

Teddy blinked. "Really?"

"I'm not a monster, Teddy. You've been more than patient. She can spend the night."

"Thank you. I appreciate that."

Dorcas gave a chuckle. "And yet you still don't trust me. See you tomorrow. I won't go back on my word." She kissed her forefinger then touched it to his cheek. "Goodnight, Teddy."

"Goodnight."

TEDDY STILL DIDN'T KNOW what to think as he drove to Jess's beach house, but all other thoughts fled his mind when he saw the police cruisers outside her place. His heart thumping heavily against his ribs, he pulled the car over and jumped out. He was stopped at Jess's doorway, and although the officer recognized him, he still asked for ID before he would let him in.

"Is Jess okay?" Teddy tried not to let the panic in him show in his voice as he dug his ID out for the officer.

"Miss Olden is fine, sir. That's great. Thanks, Mr. Hood. You're cleared." He officer nodded at him, handing back Teddy's ID and stepping aside to let him in.

Teddy saw the blood on the floor of Jess's hallway and balked. "It's not mine." He looked up to see Jess leaning against the kitchen door smiling at him, a half-empty glass of rosé in her hand. "It's courtesy of some dead rats and an anonymous asshole with a bad sense of humor."

Teddy went to her. "It's the second time today."

"I know that. It's annoying and frustrating, but nothing dangerous. Three guesses who's responsible."

"Taran Googe?"

"Bingo. Although, as a lawyer, I shouldn't say that. There's no proof, but this reeks of him. Still, let's go get you a drink. These guys are almost done, then I can clean up, and we can relax."

He followed her into the kitchen, and she snagged him a beer from the fridge. "You seem remarkably okay with all this."

"No one got hurt. It's just some petty shit by someone whose masculinity is easily bruised. Bro-douchebag, ahoy." She stroked his face. "But who cares about that? I adored DJ! What a great kid."

Teddy smiled. "She loved you, too, but then she always did take after her father. Dorcas is letting me keep her overnight tomorrow."

"Wow." Jess's eyes were huge. "That's... unexpected."

"Right? That was my first reaction."

"Huh."

"What?"

Jess shook her head. "No, nothing, just... my spidey senses are wondering why she's suddenly being so flexible."

Teddy laughed. "She's just trying to rehab her public image, and I hope, just maybe she's putting DJ first."

Jess looked skeptical, and Teddy touched her cheek, grinning. "Yeah, I know."

Jess shrugged and was silent for a while, then she gave him a steady look. "I know nothing about parenthood, but can I ask? Is it usual to give a kid vitamins?"

"Depends on the situation, but it's not unusual, why?"

"Nah, nothing." Jess waved a hand. "I was just wondering."

Teddy wasn't convinced that was the whole story, but he let it go. "Come on, let's go see if these people are done."

JESS THANKED the lead detective when the crime scene people had finished up, and he nodded to her. "We'll stay in touch, Miss Olden. We'll be following up on the tip you gave us, but we found no fingerprints and with the cameras out..."

"I understand. Thanks for your help."

Teddy was waiting for her in the living room. "What a day."

"Right?" She flopped down on the sofa next to him and smiled. "But, hey, it was a good day for the most part."

Teddy kissed the tip of her nose. "I'm glad. My two favorite girls."

Jess grinned. "Is the other one me or Dorcas?" She laughed as he tickled her.

"You might as well know," Teddy said nonchalantly, "that I'm madly in love with you, Jessica Olden."

Jess stopped laughing, but her eyes were soft. "Love isn't a word I throw around lightly."

"Me, either," he said, not looking away from her. "But I love you."

Jess's mouth curved up in a smile. "I love you, too, Teddy Hood."

His lips were against hers then, and there seemed to be no more reason to talk, just touch, and kiss, and caress.

They never made to her bed, tugging each other's clothes off and making love on the carpet, right there in her living room. Teddy's lips were urgent against hers, then as his mouth moved down her body, Jess shivered with pleasure as his tongue found her clit.

His fingers dug into the soft flesh of her inner thigh as he went down her, his tongue lashing and flicking her clit until she was ready to explode, then his tongue plunged into her vagina and she did come, crying out his name, completely undone.

He didn't give her time to recover before his thick, long cock was thrusting into her, and he began to fuck her hard, murmuring her name over and over, his smile both triumphant and utterly besotted.

Jess tightened her thighs around him, urging him deeper, kissing him, biting his lower lips in her frantic desire for him. Teddy pinned her hands to the carpet as he increased his pace, and Jess nodded, yes, yes, yes to the question in his eyes.

As she came again, she couldn't help the words that came out of her in a whisper, and it was something she had never, ever said, to anyone.

"Promise me you'll never leave me..."

Teddy kissed her tenderly. "I promise, my lovely Jessie... I promise."

CHAPTER NINETEEN – TAKE ME HOME

Los Angeles

Taran Googe had expected the visit from the police about what had happened at the offices and at Jessica's home, but he handled it, being cooperative, not denying he had a beef with her, but ultimately denying any knowledge of the incidents.

And he'd been careful. He hadn't looked up anything on the net to do with mail hoaxes, hadn't left any kind of trail. He wasn't as stupid as everyone thought he was.

Eventually, the police had to leave him alone—after all, there was no proof—and leaving dead rats in somebody's home was hardly high priority. Okay, so the powder in the envelope thing could have been considered a felony....

Taran grinned as he shut the door on the police officers. They had nothing. And to be honest, he'd had his fun. He was getting a little tired of the whole Jess Olden thing. If he'd upset her day for even a little bit, then, okay, they were even.

He went back to his bottle of scotch and the heroin he'd luckily not cooked up before the police came. A little bliss trip would be the perfect end to the perfect day—good thing they hadn't searched his apartment.

He snorted up a couple of lines and sat back, letting the drug course through his system. A half hour later, he was so blissed out, he barely heard the doorbell again. He stumbled to the door before it occurred to him it might be the police again—and he was in no fit state for them.

"Who is it?"

"A friend, Mr. Googe." A woman's voice. Clipped. Well-spoken. He opened the door.

A beautiful woman, brittle but still attractive, stood outside. Her straw-blonde hair was piled up in a bun, and she wore gloves on her hands. She certainly looked out of place in this part of town.

And she looked vaguely familiar. "May I come in?"

Taran blinked and stood aside, almost dumbfounded. Her name came to him as he followed her inside. "Dorcas Prettyman?"

She smiled at him, but it didn't reach her eyes. "I'd prefer it if you called me... Daphne. While we conduct our business."

"We have business?" Through the fog of his drug-addled brain, he was starting to make the connection. Of course. Jess Olden was fucking Teddy Hood, Dorcas's ex-husband. "Jess Olden."

Dorcas nodded and sat down, perching gingerly on the edge of the cleanest chair she could find. She kept her gloves on as she surveyed the room, then looked back at him. "I think we could be of use to each other."

Taran vaguely wondered if she would screw him to get what she wanted but pushed the thought aside. *Think straight, dude.* This bitch was loaded, and whatever she wanted with Jess Olden, it wasn't going to be friendly. Which was… interesting. He was aware he was gaping at the movie star sitting in his apartment.

"Mr. Googe?"

"Yes?"

Dorcas smiled coldly. "Would you be interested in working together?"

"Of course."

"Good. Now, perhaps you'd like to offer me a drink?"

New York State

India's reaction to the house surprised Massimo, but he kept his counsel, not wanting to get too excited. They'd begun to search again for their *forever home*, as India called it, and after a few missteps, they had found this one, out of the city, on the banks of the Hudson.

Massimo had felt it as soon as they drove along the long gravel drive to the house, and he'd glanced at India to see the excitement in her eyes, too. Because they had been disappointed in the past, they both stayed silent as the realtor showed them around, but he felt India's fingers pressing hard against his as they visited each room of the house.

As far as private mansions went, it wasn't over the top nor ostentatious, but it was large enough that they could grow into it. There was room for a recording studio in one of the outbuildings, enough guest bedrooms for all of their friends, way more bathrooms than they would ever need.

The gardens were the tipping point. Large, but with trees surrounding the property and a view down to the river, Massimo could imagine their kids running around, dogs, parties with their friends in the summer. "Man," was all he said, and India laughed. She turned to the realtor.

"We have terrible poker faces, both of us, but would you mind giving us a moment?"

The realtor laughed and nodded. "Of course."

Massimo smiled down at India. "Yes?" was all he said, and she nodded.

"It's the place, isn't it?"

"One hundred percent." Massimo looked around the grounds again and wrapped his arms around his love. "It's our home, isn't it?"

India nodded, and he saw tears in her eyes. "Hey, hey."

India chuckled. "Happy tears, I swear. I never thought we'd find somewhere. God, this garden..."

"I know."

They stood in silence for a few minutes, drinking in the scene. "Baby?"

"Yes, beautiful?"

"I think I'd like to get married here in the garden. It's so perfect. We could put twinkle lights in the streets, hang paper lanterns. That pergola, we could drape flowers over it and get married under it...do you think Sun and Tae would like it?"

Sun and Tae were getting married alongside their friends in America, because South Korea didn't recognize gay marriage yet, and they were trying to decide on a venue. "I think they would."

"If not, I don't mind, but God, this place." India's face was glowing, and Massimo had thought she had never looked more beautiful than in this moment.

"I love you, India Blue."

She turned in his arms and stroked his face. "And I you, Massi. I keep meaning to tell you that I'm so proud of the way you've been working on yourself, you know. The psychologist really seems to be working out for you."

Massimo chuckled softly. "I won't deny it was hard at first. I'm a provincial guy, Indy. My dad would never have seen a psychologist... so yeah, it was difficult. Dumb male ego, but now... yeah, I think I could have, *should have*, done this a long time ago. I lost my dad, then almost lost you in such short order. It was dumb to think that wouldn't have some kind of kick back."

India smiled at him. "It helped me... and I'm sorry. I should have suggested a long time ago."

"I'm a big boy, Indy. Now, let's go buy our dream home."

BACK AT HIS MANHATTAN APARTMENT, Massimo and India showered together, making love in the hot running water, and then Massimo dressed and went to call his agent and publicist, Jake. The film with Teddy Hood was greenlit, and they'd be filming the next couple of months.

India waited until she heard Massimo talking to Jake, and then went back into the bathroom, opening the cabinet under the sink and pulling out a brown paper bag. Inside, she fished out the pregnancy test. Her period had not come; she was two weeks late. and now she was convinced that she was indeed carrying Massimo's child. She felt different, had been feeling different for weeks now, but with Massimo doing so well with his mood and his depression, she had wanted to be absolutely sure before she said anything. The first few tests she had taken had turned up negative, but she wasn't discouraged. She knew it took time to find out if she was.

Today, though, she was confident. Today, what with them finding the house, it just seemed inevitable. She took the test out of the packet and sat down on the toilet to take it.

India jiggled her legs up and down as she waited for the test to complete. If she was pregnant, that would mean she would still be so when they got married, but it didn't matter. That would make it all the more perfect.

She counted down the three minutes and picked up the stick.

Negative.

"No, come on, now." She snagged another one from the bag and retook it. "You better work, I'm running out of pee." She set the new test down and returned to the old. Was there a faint line? She couldn't tell if she was imagining it.

She didn't hear Massimo return to the bathroom until he spoke, and she nearly jumped out of her skin when she heard his voice. "Piccolo?"

She turned guiltily and grinned. "Don't get excited, but I really think this time…"

Massimo's eyes were unreadable. "Darling…"

She picked up the first stick. "Excuse the fact I peed on this, but there's a faint line, right?"

Massimo held the stick and studied it. "Honestly, I don't see it, baby."

"Okay," she was a little frustrated. Why wasn't he more excited? "I'm retaking it in case it's a dud, but Massi, I'm almost two weeks late."

"You didn't tell me."

"We've had false alarms before, honey." Her phone began to ring incessantly, but she ignored it. "But my body *feels* different. Weirdly swollen, and my breasts have been hurting."

"You didn't say."

"Not enough to be anything but annoying, but my body is changing. And I'm sure I've put on weight."

Massimo grinned then. "Fatty. But, seriously, if anything, you were thinner than you should be, not surprisingly after what happened. You always had the most gorgeous, breakneck curves when I met you... it's just returning to that after everything. You're nowhere in the region of fat." He seemed to realize that wasn't what she wanted to hear and took her in his arms. "But it could mean we have a little one on the way, too. Don't think I'm being negative."

"You want kids, right?"

"I do. I want a hundred little Indy's running around. God, answer your phone, please! It's driving me insane."

It was Lazlo, India's older brother and manager. "Hey, Boo! Listen, are you in the city?"

"I am, what's up?"

Lazlo told her one of the late night guys had called, telling Lazlo he had a guest cancel and he was wondering if India would fill the slot.

"Tonight?" India had been out of the loop for so long when it came to public appearances that she felt a little panicky at the thought.

"You can say no, but you'd be doing me a favor. I owe Jimmy one."

India tried not to sigh, then felt guilty. Lazlo worked his ass off for her, and he'd been making sure her fans were informed at every level of her recovery, shielding her from the worst intrusive journalists. She owed him. "Tell him yes. I can be at the studio in an hour."

She said goodbye to Lazlo and told Massimo what was up. He nodded. "I can come with you."

She grinned at him, knowing he was going into protective mode. "Honey, only come if you're prepared to come on set with me, because if you show up in the green room, there's no way they won't drag you on screen."

Massimo shrugged. "Let them. We don't have to hide anymore, right?"

India smiled. "You're right. Let me call Laz back, and we can tell them it'll be a joint appearance for the first time. Better we don't have time to think about it."

She drew in a deep breath then and picked up the second stick. Disappointment flooded her system. "Oh." Negative. She looked at Massimo, who cradled her face in his arms.

"We have forever, baby girl. There's no rush. Let's not get sad about things we can't change."

"You're right." God, she loved this man with her whole heart. He had saved her in so many ways. "Now, let's go get ready for our debut performance."

Los Angeles

Jess had spent the afternoon with Teddy and DJ again, this time at her beach house, and she'd made up a bedroom for DJ, finding herself loving choosing the little touches. A stack of books on the night stand, a special nightlight—a small Moon with the correct geographical features for the geek in DJ, and DJ had loved it.

"If you come again," Jess said, blushing furiously at the girl's delight, "we could decorate the whole room how you want it."

"Could we make a den?"

"Of course! We could do that tomorrow. I'm sure I have enough things for it already."

DJ smiled shyly at her. "Thank you, Jessie. Will you lay in it with me and read?"

"I would love that."

When DJ had settled down for a nap before supper, Teddy and Jess went out onto the deck, sharing a bottle of wine, listening to the ocean. Teddy pulled Jess onto his lap, and she wound her arm around his shoulders. "I love you, and I love your kid, Mr. Hood."

Teddy kissed her. "Is it wrong to say that I wish more than anything that you were DJ's Mommy? That this was our little family?" He sighed, leaning his head against hers. "In this lovely place with the ocean just there. All we need is…"

"A dog." They said it together and laughed. Jess smoothed his hair back from his face.

"Listen, how about we take DJ to the pound—"

"—CPS would really frown upon that."

"Ha ha, silly man. I meant, we should all go pick out a pup. I did think before that I couldn't have a dog because I work all day... but then again, it's my company so I can take the pup into the office with me."

"Or when I'm home... I mean, here," To her surprise, Teddy flushed, then grinned. "Sorry, but I do think of this as home now."

"Then why don't we make it official? Move in. It's not grand, but it's home."

"It is, it really is. I will, thank you."

"Then we can definitely decorate DJ's room."

Teddy chuckled. "You're desperate for that reading den, aren't you?"

"I am, I really am." Jess nuzzled her nose against his. "We could always build one in our room, for things other than reading."

"Unless it's the *Kama Sutra*."

"Well, yes." Her phone bleeped, and she read the message. "Oh, wow. Looks like Massi and Indy are making their public debut as a couple on the late show tonight. Want to watch?"

"Sure. After dinner."

JESS HAD ORDERED pizza for them, and she and Teddy sat with DJ as they ate, chatting and laughing. She had ordered DJ's favorite pizza, double pepperoni with pineapple, which made Teddy make a disgusted face, and she and Teddy shared a cheese pizza with chili peppers liberally scattered across it.

Finally, DJ was drooping, and they put her to bed

together; DJ wanted Jess to come read to her. Jess felt her heart pound with love for the little girl and for the easy way she had welcomed Jess into her life. She was so loving, so bright and warm, that Jess wondered if her no-kids rule had been so misplaced all these years.

It also made her question her own childhood. Clearly, she did not have the normal childhood that most kids— most kids?—had, but it made her resent her father even more. To think we could have had this, she thought looking at the bond between Teddy and DJ. It made her sad.

But later, when she and Teddy had settled down to watch India and Massimo on the late show, she felt guilty. At least her father had never tried to kill her, unlike India's psychopathic politician dad. Jess had spent a year putting Philip LeFevre behind bars for life for it. She had wondered over the years whether she should try and make her father pay for what he had done to Katie, but the truth was, she was done with him. She wanted nothing to do with the man anymore, and the fact Taran Googe had dragged him back to her attention was an annoyance, sure, but at least it had gone no further. She didn't want her Dad back in her life. Ever.

India and Massi were doing well in their first joint interview, both warm and funny, but Jess knew India of old —she could tell she was nervous.

"They're a sweet couple." Teddy's voice broke into her thoughts and she blinked, then smiled at him.

"They really are. You're going to have a blast working

with Massimo. I don't know Tiger Rose well, but she seems like a great girl, too."

"I'm looking forward to it. I really am." Teddy gave a sigh. "After the last year and a half, I feel like things are finally getting settled." He stroked the back of his finger down her cheek. "And better than I ever could have imagined."

Jess smiled at him and was about to answer him when they heard the scream. In a second they were both up and running towards DJ's room.

DJ had thrown up all over her comforter, and to Jess's horror, there was blood mixed into the vomit. Teddy swept his daughter up and carried her to the bathroom, where DJ threw up again.

"Sweetheart?"

But DJ was too sick to talk, and when Jess swept a hand onto her forehead, she was burning up. "Teddy we need to call a paramedic... I have no medicine here for her." Jess felt like crying when she saw the distress on Teddy's face, and her heart was aching for DJ, who was sobbing now, in pain.

"Teddy, let's take her to the emergency room." Jess was already grabbing her keys as Teddy brought DJ through, wrapped in a blanket.

"I'm sorry I threw up on your bed," DJ was crying, and Jess kissed her hot forehead.

"Darling, it's okay. I just want you to feel better. Come on, I'll drive."

CHAPTER TWENTY – AM I WRONG

Los Angeles

A FEW HOURS LATER, the doctor had examined DJ and given her an anti-emetic and a sedative, and she was sleeping fitfully. Teddy had called Dorcas who came right away and ignored Jess mostly, but didn't ask for her to leave.

Jess watched Dorcas carefully. She still wasn't convinced Dorcas wasn't behind DJ's continued illness, but she questioned herself if that wasn't because she felt terribly guilty that DJ got ill at her own home. Still, she couldn't shake her suspicions, especially when Dorcas seemed to snag the attention of every staff member, whether they were treating DJ or not.

Jess went down to get coffee for all of them later that night, and saw Dorcas talking with a small press pack that she must have called. Jess tried to hear what she was saying but couldn't get close enough. It irked her though, and her irritation must have shown on her face when she returned to Teddy's side. He took the coffee from her, but his eyes raked her face. "What's up?"

She told him about the press pack, and he rolled his eyes. "That's just Dorcas. As long as she keeps them away from DJ, and doesn't spin them a web of lies, I can't care about that at the moment."

"Hmm."

Teddy smiled at her. "Momma Bear. It's okay."

DJ's doctor came to see Teddy, explaining that they were looking at something DJ may have ingested as they found no viral or bacterial reason for her sickness. "She was sweaty and clammy, for sure, but her actual body temperature was normal. What did she eat this evening?"

They told the doctor, and he nodded. "Well, that's benign enough... can I ask, where you were eating, where there any plants or shrubs nearby?"

"No, it's just a deck. The house is on the beach, and I kill any plants I try to keep." Jess winced at her own words, but both Teddy and the doctor didn't seem phased. "Doc," Jess decided to brave the question. "Is there such a thing as vitamin poisoning?"

"Sure, and we'll test for that, too, but to be honest, the symptoms don't match up with that and it's very, very difficult to achieve without detection. DJ's blood results will show us more. I'll be back later."

Teddy looked at Jess after the doctor had gone. "Where were you going with that question?" There was an edge to his voice, and Jess knew he hadn't missed the implication in her words.

"Teddy... don't you think it's strange DJ keeps getting sick? And that when she does, Dorcas gets a shit ton of publicity? Not to mention attention from the staff here."

Teddy's eyes never left her face, but he was silent for a long moment. Then, she saw the anger crackling in him as he stood up. "I don't want to ever hear you talk like that again. Understood? Dorcas is a lot of things, but she would never, ever hurt DJ. *Ever.*"

His tone was surprisingly calm, but his blue eyes were colder than she had ever seen. But Jess, mindful of DJ's health, didn't back down. "The question needs to be asked, Teddy, Too many things don't add up. Why is DJ constantly sick?"

"Jesus. It could be any number of things, Jess, do you know how many times kids get sick from the slightest thing? She could have picked something up from another kid."

"They've already said it isn't viral or bacterial."

"So you, great detective that you are, have decided Dorcas is poisoning her?"

"What better way to keep you close."

Teddy gaped at her, opened his mouth, then shut it, and passed a hand over his face. Jess waited for the explosion, but it never came. She wasn't sorry she had pushed it —Teddy needed to have the suspicion planted in his brain, just so he could consider it in the great scheme of things.

Whatever the cost.

"I think you need to go now," Teddy said, but his tone was gentle. "I need to be with my daughter."

"Of course." Jess felt her heart thump with sadness, but she could understand why he was asking her to leave. "You will let me know if anything changes."

Teddy half-smiled. "Of course." He didn't attempt to kiss her goodbye, but Jess went to DJ's side and kissed the little girl's forehead, and he didn't stop her.

"Be well, bunny," she whispered to the sleeping child and touched Teddy's hand as she left.

She waited until she had driven at least a few miles away from the hospital before she burst into tears.

New York

INDIA WAS STILL awake at two a.m. when her cell phone bleeped with a message.

Hey, Boo, are you still awake? I need some girl talk and advice. J x

India slid out of bed, careful not to wake the sleeping Massimo, and went out into the living room. It was cold, and she snagged an oversized purple chenille throw and grabbed a bottle of water before she snuggled into the sofa and called Jess back. "Hey, girl, what's up?"

She listened as Jess told her all about Teddy's kid and the argument they'd had. "Do you think I was right to question the vitamin thing, Indy? Or is that my experience with bad parents coming through..?"

"Probably both. Hey look, at the end of the day, the most important thing is that the kid is okay. Do you like her?"

"I love her. I *love* her, Indy. I wish she was mine." Jess sounded a little drunk, and Indy wasn't surprised. Jess didn't drink much, but she did when she was genuinely upset. "I hated seeing her so sick."

Indy thought she heard a little sob. "Oh, sweetie, don't cry."

"I'm not crying, I burped," Jess protested in an outraged voice, but Indy could tell she was lying. "I just love that kid, she's so special, Indy, and I want to know what's going on with her. I know Dorcas Prettyman, and I wouldn't put it past her to hurt DJ for attention."

"You're talking about Munchausen's by proxy?"

"Yes. How do you know about it?"

"Ha. With my family? There's not many psychological disorders I don't know about. After my dad and everything, when I was in therapy, I got obsessed with trying to find reason why he would want me dead, why he would pay someone to kill me. *Twice*."

"Did you get an answer?" Jess hiccupped softly again, and Indy half-smiled.

"Kind of. He has Asshole Disease."

They both laughed quietly. "Amen to that." Jess was quiet for a moment. "I know her. Dorcas. She's a vile piece of shit regardless of how she's trying to rehab her image. It is, and always has been, all about her. Teddy and DJ—they are just extensions of her. Accessories."

"Jessie?"

"Yeah?"

"Are you morphing Dorcas and your dad together?"

Jess sighed. "Well, that's my question. Am I? I don't know. I can't get clarity."

"And Teddy wouldn't entertain the notion?"

"Nope."

"But it's like *Objection, Sustained*, but the jury still heard it?"

"Yup."

India smiled. "Always the lawyer."

Jess sighed. "I don't know. I hope I haven't blown it, but as you say, the priority is DJ. If it turns out I'm right, but Teddy still hates me, if it means DJ is okay, then I'm okay with that." She didn't sound okay with that at all. She cleared her throat. "Oh hey, I saw your segment on the show. You and Massimo look so great together... if you could act, boo, we'd have a new screen Golden Couple."

"Ha, no thanks." India sighed. "I enjoyed it, and it took my mind off the fact that I'm still not pregnant."

Jess had been the only person she's confided her hopes to over the last month, and now she heard Jess sigh. "I'm sorry, boo. But, listen, I know it's been almost two years, but the trauma to your body... you're still healing. There's no rush."

"That's what Massi said, and I know you're both right... I was disappointed, is all."

"Listen... Lazlo called me the other day. He wants you to get back to work, so what about that?"

India laughed. "Ha, he told me that, too. He's right, I need to get back out there. I want to do some stuff with Sun and Tae..."

"Ha, I bet you do."

"*Music* stuff, you pervert," India laughed. They chatted for a while longer, then as they were saying goodbye, India asked her if she was sure about Teddy. "I know you're in love with him... but how well do you really know their relationship? I don't want you getting hurt between two people who can't figure out their shit."

"Which reminds, how is Valentina?"

They both laughed. "Very much out of the picture, thank God. Listen... we found a house."

"At freaking last."

"So, the wedding's going to be there, and I want Teddy Hood on your arm at my wedding."

"Show off."

"Yup. Anyway, I think you did the right thing. I *think* you did. I'm no expert, of course."

Jess chuckled. "You made me feel better, and I can't thank you enough for that. It's been a rough day and a half, what with this and the Taran Googe anthrax stuff."

India's heart pounded hard. "What damn anthrax stuff? What the hell?"

Jess sighed. "Oh, that's a story. Strap yourself in, this might take some time."

Los Angeles

Dorcas had called him and told him that Jess was at the hospital with Teddy and DJ and that her home was clear. Taran had managed to keep himself sober for one night—although the temptation of the high quality drugs Dorcas was paying him in was almost unbearable. So he jumped into his car, drove out to Jess's neighborhood. He parked a couple of blocks away as always and headed down to the beach to make his approach from there.

By now, he knew every corner of Jess Olden's home, even the tricky door out to the deck. After he'd climbed up on the deck, he tried it and found it open. Really, Jess, all this security and then there's this back hole right here? He snuck inside, his backpack on his shoulder. Inside it was high-end surveillance recording equipment that Dorcas's money had bought him. Dorcas wanted every minute of Jess's life documented. Every moment.

Taran was looking forward to seeing Jess fucking Teddy Hood. He'd been obsessing over her sensational body since that first time he'd watched them. He headed for her bedroom first and set up the equipment as discreet as he could imagine. Jess Olden wasn't someone who had much in the way of furry toys to hide cameras in—not a surprise for a thirty-five-year-old woman, but he managed to come up with a couple of ideas.

He was just securing a camera in the living room in the leaves of a potted plant when he heard her car in the driveway. Shit. He headed towards the door then realized his backpack was still in her bedroom.

Fuck...

He darted back into her room, but then heard her come in the door. He was trapped. He crammed himself into the closet, covering himself with some clothes that were at the bottom of it. It was a shitty disguise, and if she was paying attention, she would find him in a hot minute, but...

If he had to hurt her to get out of there, so be it. He would. He could hurt her... right? He rummaged gingerly in his bag, but there was nothing he could use as a weapon. Damn it.

Taran remained squashed into the closet, but Jess never even came to the bedroom. After a couple of hours, he heard her talking on the phone for a while. She and Teddy had had some kind of argument and when he heard what she suspected about Dorcas, he nearly crowed in delight. Dorcas would want to know what her ex-husband's new girlfriend thought of her.

Dorcas? Hurting her own kid? Actually, he could well believe it, but that wasn't his most pressing concern right now.

After a while, the house was quiet, and he heard Jess coming to the bedroom, getting ready for bed. Through the slats in the closet door, he watched her get undressed, then head to the bathroom to shower and brush her teeth. Seems she liked to sleep naked even when Teddy Hood wasn't with her.

He waited for her to get into bed and switch off the lamp on her nightstand. He listened to her sleep for a while, his cock at full mast thinking of her naked body only a foot away from him.

When he was sure she was asleep, he pushed open the door of the closet gently and crawled out. He made it to the kitchen before he heard her voice.

"I have a gun, motherfucker, and it's aimed right at your back. You have five seconds to get out or I'll use it."

Taran smiled to himself. He knew she didn't have a gun —he'd combed every drawer and cupboard in her place. His eye was drawn to the knife block on the counter. He could have a little fun...the darkness would hide his face, right?

Moving quickly, he grabbed the biggest knife from the block and swung around... and Jess fired a shot. Fuck. She *did* have a gun.

"Three... two..."

Taran scooted around and crashed out of the backdoor onto the deck, jumping back down on the sand and running in case Jess got off another shot. Jesus. He nearly fucked everything up. He got into his car and drove home, hoping like hell he wouldn't get another visit from the police.

Instead, he got high on the drugs Dorcas had given him and waited for her to call and tell him what she wanted to do next.

JESS SMILED SHEEPISHLY at the detective, the same one who had been dealing with her for the last twenty-four hours, but he didn't smile back. "Miss Olden... we think it's probably time to take your security seriously."

"I know. I have some people coming out."

"Is Mr. Hood not here?"

Jess raised her eyebrows at him, and he smiled. "I don't mean I don't think you're capable of looking after yourself. God forbid. My wife would hear that from here and beat my ass."

His smile faded. "But someone is targeting you, and we take stalking very seriously. He's already ramped it up by being here when you are home. We saw the knife on the floor. He could have killed you. Is there somewhere you can go?"

Jess sighed. "I can go to a hotel."

"Good. We can have a car take you if you would like."

"No, I'll take a cab. Just give me a half hour to pack a bag."

CHAPTER TWENTY-ONE – BIG GIRLS CRY

Los Angeles

IN THE CAR ride to the hotel—and she had picked one close to the hospital where DJ was—she called Teddy, hoping he would take her call after their argument earlier. She felt a rush of relief when he did. "Hey, how's DJ?"

"Doing okay. Not great, but okay. They still don't know what's causing it. You okay?"

She told him about the break-in and was touched when he sounded as shocked and worried as she felt. "I'm going to the hotel next to the hospital... in case you need me or need a place to crash close by." She hesitated. God what was it about this man that made her feel like a nervous teenager? "I packed some fresh clothes and toiletries for you. No biggie but just in case."

She heard him sigh. "Sweetheart, I'm sorry I got angry earlier."

"It's okay, it was insensitive of me to start in on, well, you know. I love you, I love DJ, and I'm so worried about her."

"I know. Me, too. I just can't fathom that Dorcas would... God, that's so fucking sick."

"I know."

"Look, DJ is asleep, and Dorcas is staying with her tonight. How about I meet you at the hotel and we can talk?"

"I would like that."

AN HOUR later and Jess heard his soft knock on her room door. She opened it and saw his shattered face, his exhaustion. "Oh, baby." She took his hand and pulled him inside. He let her hug him tightly, seeming to need it desperately. "I don't think talking is what you need right now. Food, coffee and sleep, maybe."

"I have to agree, that sounds perfect."

Jess ordered a very early breakfast for them both, and while they were waiting, they took a shower together. She poured him some fresh coffee from the pot as they ate scrambled eggs and pancakes.

She took him to bed afterward, and he wanted to make love even though he was almost dropping with fatigue. "I need to be close to you," he said, and Jess kissed him, wrapping her legs around him as he pushed inside her.

They made love slowly, their eyes never leaving the others as they kiss, caressed. Fatigue had set in and neither of them came hard, just a gentle release of tension, and then Teddy fell asleep wrapped in her arms.

Despite her own tiredness, Jess couldn't sleep. What a twenty-four hours. She closed her eyes and tried to drop off but found herself thinking of what might have been. If she hadn't woken and heard the douchebag creeping around in her home. The way he grabbed that knife... was he there to kill her?

She somehow didn't think so, but then why was he there? If it was Googe, again, what the hell was he thinking? Was it really worth jailtime to torment her? *The fucker.*

But there was a creeping paranoia in her that it wasn't Googe, that it was someone more insidious, someone more dangerous than an idiot guy from the internet.

When sleep finally came, the nightmares did, too. She dreamed of her friends laying slaughtered, imagine India being murdered by Braydon Carter, Coco dropping dead right in front of her. Alex taking his own life. Massimo throwing himself from a building after India's death. Sun and Tae dead, wrapped in each other's arms.

Teddy, his eyes open and staring as Dorcas stood above him with a smoking gun. DJ in a tiny coffin.

Katie...

Jess didn't realize she was screaming until she felt Teddy's arms around her, and in her panic, she tried to escape him, but he held her tightly, talking to her in a calm, soothing voice until she calmed down.

Eventually the panic subsided, and she slumped against him. "I'm sorry. Bad dreams."

"Tell me."

Jess swallowed hard, and Teddy reached over to pass her a bottle of water. "Take a breath, have some water, and talk to me, baby."

She did as she was told, sipping the water, taking deep breaths until she could speak. She told him about the dream, about her friends dying, editing out the part about him and DJ.

Teddy stroked her damp hair away from her forehead. "Katie was your sister?"

She nodded. "My younger sister by five years. We were so close, Teddy. I thought we knew absolutely everything about each other. We looked after each other when it came to Dad's emotional abuse; we knew he was an asshole, but until one of us was eighteen and able to support ourselves, we were trapped. When I turned eighteen, I tried to get legal custody of Katie, but Dad had his hand in many, many pies in our town. I was laughed out of court. I went to college close by so that Katie could stay with me in the dorms as much as possible."

Jess sighed and leaned against Teddy's hard chest. "Then, one day, I had a call to go see the Dean. Katie had jumped from the apartment building next to ours. Fourteen stories, she didn't stand a chance. The next day I got her letter."

Teddy didn't say anything, but she felt his arms tighten around her, and knew he realized what she was about to say. But she needed to say it, needed to tell the person she loved most in the world—and that was shocking to her—to hear her truth. "Our father had been raping her for years, since before I'd even left home. She never said a word and I had no idea. *No* idea. How could I not have known?"

She took another breath. "So I went to the police, of course I did, and... nothing. Nothing was done and the letter up and disappeared. Imagine that. The fuckers. So... I guess what I'm trying to say that my sensors are up when it comes to child abuse. I admit, I sometimes see it where it doesn't exist. I'm sorry about what I said about Dorcas. I have no proof, just an instinct. But I'm prepared to admit I was wrong to say it without any evidence."

Teddy kissed her temple. "Don't worry about it. I love that you care enough about DJ to want to protect her. You've only met her twice and already..." His voice drifted off and she looked at him curiously.

"What?"

Teddy shook his head. "It's just... when I see you two together, I can't believe you haven't known each other for ever. I see more warmth between you than I've seen between my daughter and my ex-wife for a long, long time."

"What was Dorcas like when DJ was born?"

Teddy chewed his lip. "I never had any doubt that she loved DJ, but it still seemed like she felt she was inconvenienced by the whole thing. She didn't breastfeed, and not that it's anything to be ashamed of, but she didn't even *try*. Said she didn't want her nipples to be 'misshapen' and poke through her couture."

Jess snorted at his expression. "Well, it's not for everyone. But she loves DJ, right?"

"I think so." But he didn't look convinced. "Her having used her as a pawn to try and get me back hasn't helped her case."

"Still, it was wrong of me to accuse her of harming DJ when I had no proof. I'm glad she didn't hear me."

"She didn't mention anything when she came back from the myriad of press interviews."

Jess kissed him. "Am I forgiven?"

"Of course. God, I love you, Jessie. Even when you make me mad."

"I seem to have a gift for that."

Teddy grinned. "It's a gift, all right. Look, changing the subject, I meant what I said about moving in with you, but we seriously have to talk about upping your security."

Jess sighed. "I know. I have been slack, there's no arguing with that. I will get to it, I promise."

"I hope you don't mind, but I kind of sent some security expert out to your place. I panicked."

Jess smiled at him. "No, it's okay, thank you. Better to get it done."

Teddy held her, pressing his lips to her temple. "You think it's Googe?"

"Honestly, I don't know. He doesn't seem like the type

to actually hurt someone, you know, he seems too much like a wuss to do that. Keying my car and leaving dead rats, yes. Actually causing physical harm? I don't know."

LATER, they learned from the police that Taran Googe had been questioned formally, but released without charge for the break-in, at least. He'd been cautioned over possession of a small amount of heroin that they had found at his place, but it was so miniscule, they said, that it would cost more to prosecute him than it was worth.

Teddy rolled his eyes. "Let's hope he gets his hands on some more and overdoses on that shit. I have no sympathy."

Jess was at a loss to wonder who would hate her so much that they would break in. Teddy came with her back to her home, and they found that now anyone would find it hard to get in. Teddy looked as relieved as Jess felt. He stroked a hand down her back. "And I'll be here now."

She smiled up at him. "You'll still move in?"

"Of course, baby. I love you."

Jess leaned against his hard chest. "We should decorate the guest room for DJ."

"That would be nice."

But an hour later they got the call from the hospital. DJ was in a coma.

. . .

Dorcas listened to the doctor, nodding her head, playing her part well. DJ was pale and clammy as she lay comatose in the bed, and Dorcas made a show of weeping gently, holding her daughter's hand.

Her heart was thumping though. She hadn't meant it to get this far, but it was what it was. The doctors were stymied, and she judged them for not thinking outside the box, although she was glad they did.

She asked her publicist to come to the hospital and work on a press statement, and then she waited for Teddy to arrive. When he did, Dorcas felt a flash of pure anger that Jessica Olden was holding hands with him, but this wasn't the time nor place for jealousy.

"Darling." She went to Teddy immediately, beginning to sob, deftly extracting him from Jess's hold. Teddy patted her back awkwardly.

"How is she?"

"She won't wake up, Ted. Ted... what if our little girl dies?" She sobbed harder until Teddy was forced to put his arms around her and steer her into a chair. Dorcas was surprised when Jess took her hand, murmuring comfort to her. Surprised and resentful. Dorcas should be the one to show compassion... Jess Olden was seriously getting on her last nerve.

As they talked and sat with DJ, she watched them together; she noticed how they had oriented themselves around each other, their body language, the way they mirrored each other. Dorcas hated to admit it, but she and Teddy had never had this, this closeness, the way he and

Jess seemed not only to be lovers, but best friends, two halves of one being.

Yeah, Jess Olden was more than an inconvenience. Dorcas looked away, glancing up at the TV that flickered silently on the wall. She raised her eyebrows when she saw Jess's face on the screen. "What's this about?"

Jess looked up and groaned. "Jesus. Nothing, really. Someone broke into my home last night, is all. Probably this moronic YouTuber called Taran Googe. He has a vendetta against me because I turned him down. It's nothing."

Dorcas hid a smile. Good. Taran Googe was doing what she had asked for him. Torment Jess, scare her off. Maybe it was time to ramp up the campaign. An accident, a random assault. There was something appealing about the thought of seeing Jess Olden hurt. Would Teddy's focus be split? Or would he be forced to choose between Jess and his daughter?

Or what if... What if he didn't have that choice? What if... Jess was out of the picture... permanently?

"Dorcas?"

Dorcas looked up to see Jess looking at her. "Yes?"

"Would you like some coffee?"

"No, thank you."

Jess nodded and left the room. Dorcas looked at Teddy. "Do you really think it was appropriate to bring your girlfriend to our daughter's hospital room?"

"Jess is my partner, Dorcas, whether you like it or not. She's invested. She and DJ get along great, so I think it's best if you just get used to it." Teddy's voice was firm, his eyes registering caution to her. Damn, when he was like this...

How did she ever let him get away?

Yeah... Jess Olden was going to have to go. "Excuse me for a moment. I need to make a call."

"Of course."

She went to the nearest stairwell, listened for anyone else around, but it was silent. She pulled out the burner phone she used to call Taran Googe and pressed the call button. Googe answered straight away.

"Daphne."

"Mr. Googe, I see you broke into her home?"

"Yup, and nearly got myself shot for the pleasure. I owe her some payback."

Dorcas smiled. "Good... because that's exactly what I want to give you. Let me explain what I need you to do now, and how rich I'm going to make you..."

CHAPTER TWENTY-TWO – ALL NIGHT

Los Angeles

JESS RETURNED with two steaming cups of coffee to find Teddy alone. "Where's Dorcas?"

"Making a call."

Jess kissed the top of Teddy's head. "I'm just going to use the bathroom. You okay?"

"As much as I can be."

Jess slipped out of the room and went to the ladies' restroom. As she was washing her hands, Dorcas appeared from another cubicle and nodded at her. "Jessica."

Jess gave her a half-smile. "Dorcas, you can call me Jess; it's not like we won't be seeing a lot of each other from now on."

"Rub my nose in it." Dorcas's face creased a little before she smoothed it out and she sighed. "But I have to admit… you make him happy."

"Thank you."

Dorcas dug in her purse for her lipstick, and she studied Jess's bare face in the mirror. "You know, I wouldn't be seen dead without make-up in public."

Jess bit back a retort, knowing Dorcas was trying to get a rise out of her. "All I care about is DJ." *Ooh*, low blow, but Dorcas deserved it. Dorcas harrumphed as she turned, probably to give Jess a piece of her mind, and her hand caught her purse, perched precariously on the sink, and the bag went flying, scattering its contents across the floor.

Jess helped Dorcas gather up her belongings: make-up, money, tissues, bottles of eye drops, sunglasses. Man, she was so high maintenance. Jess wondered again how on Earth her lovely, uncomplicated, feet-on-the-ground Teddy could ever have ended up with someone like Dorcas.

"Here," she said, handing Dorcas a handful of her possessions.

"Thank you." A begrudging thanks, and Jess tried not to roll her eyes. She nodded and headed for the door before Dorcas called her back. "Listen, I don't want to be an asshole… but this really should be family time."

"If Teddy wants me here, I'll stay, Dorcas."

"Fine. I'm fine with that. I'm just saying."

. . .

They both went back to DJ's room, and Teddy immediately got up and hugged Jess. They all sat waiting for the rest of the night, but in the morning Jess's phone bleeped with a message. She looked at Teddy apologetically. "I'm sorry, honey, but I'm due in court at ten for a client. I need to go home and change."

Teddy kissed her. "Of course, baby. Call me when you get out. You okay getting home on your own?"

Jess grinned at him. "You betcha."

She went down to the parking garage to find her car, running through her morning schedule in her head. She would much rather cancel and stay with Teddy, but this was an important court date for another client of hers, who was divorcing her abusive husband, and Jess would not let her down.

She clicked the lock on her car key and leaned forward to open the driver door. Jess heard the step behind her in the split second before something hard was brought down on her head; there was a blinding flash of searing pain and everything went dark.

Teddy shifted in his chair, his eyes never leaving his comatose daughter. DJ's skin was so pale and her breathing so shallow that he could barely believe she was still alive. He could feel Dorcas's eyes on him and when he looked up, he saw she had tears pouring down her cheeks.

Reluctantly he reached over and took her hand. Dorcas's fingers tangled with his immediately. "What if I did something wrong?" She whispered it so softly he could hardly hear her. "What if DJ got into something she shouldn't have?"

Teddy studied his ex-wife. "The tox screen came back negative for opioids, Dor. Are you using again?"

She shook her head. "No, I swear I'm not. Not for a long time, since before we split." She smiled a little sheepishly. "The most I do now is the odd joint, and neither of us are strangers to that."

"Marijuana wouldn't do this." He looked back at DJ, ignoring Dorcas's jibe. "What about your guests? Boyfriends?"

"There's been no one since you."

Teddy didn't believe that—there had been plenty of other men during their marriage, so why not now? He couldn't be bothered to argue. "What about the gardens? Anything there DJ could have ingested, even by mistake? Oleander?"

"The doctors already asked me, and I had someone, an expert, go over everything on the grounds. There's nothing poisonous there." She sighed, stroking DJ's soft, damp cheek. "What if it's not anything she ate or drank. What if it's something they just haven't diagnosed yet?"

"We'll find out, but they are convinced it's some kind of poison." Teddy rubbed his eyes. "But there's so many they just have to test for the right one."

"They've taken enough blood."

Teddy nodded and sat back. He was exhausted, and he already missed Jess's calming presence. He checked his watch. Ten a.m. She would be walking into court now, maybe standing for the judge, fighting for her client. God, he loved everything about her, but his very favorite thing was how much she *got* him, always. She truly was his person.

"Teddy, you look done in. They've set up a cot next door, for either of us if we needed it. Why don't you go lie down for an hour? I promise I'll wake you if anything changes."

Teddy was ready to object, but the fatigue was getting to him, and he eventually nodded and went next door.

He lay down on the cot, pulling the thin blanket over him and closing his eyes. After ten minutes, he sighed, not able to fall asleep. Instead, he remembered a night a few weeks ago, when he and Jess had been together.

They had been out to dinner with Massimo and India at one of LA's most popular restaurants, and so they'd had fans coming up to them all night for selfies and autographs. For once, none of them had minded, just grateful for the people who had made them a success in their chosen careers.

They drank mimosas and enjoyed lobster, and then went to Venice Beach. At nightfall, the beach ignited into a carnival of characters: fire-eaters, evangelicals preaching, tourists. Teddy held Jess's hand as they strolled through the throng, and they stopped to watch some of the street performers. Massimo and India were already kissing, in their own world, and Teddy and Jess exchanged an amused look. Their friends had weathered another storm, another blip in their relationship, and it gave them both hope that true love did indeed conquer any crisis.

By the time they said goodbye to Massi and India, Teddy was dying to get Jess alone and naked. They went back to her home, and as soon as Jess closed the door behind them, they were on each other, tearing at their clothes, laughing and joking as they kissed their way to her bedroom. They fell on the bed together, Teddy covering her body with his, his hands already caressing her skin. He slipped his hand between her legs and found her already wet. She grinned up at him. "I've been thinking about fucking you all night long," she purred softly. "Don't wait, Teddy, I want you inside me."

Teddy laughed, desire flooding his system. "You don't have to ask me twice, beautiful girl."

He hitched her legs around his hips and thrust hard inside her, pinning her hands above her head, his lips rough on hers. Jess's teeth bit into his hard delts painfully, but it gave him a thrill, and they got increasingly feral in their lovemaking as the night wore on.

It was probably the most uninhibited they had been with each other that night, neither holding anything back. They fucked on the floor, in the shower, clawing, biting, and knowing they would leave bruises, but neither caring.

Teddy relived every moment of the night now: the feel

of her soft skin under his, the look of love in her dark eyes as she gazed up at him, the faint red flush of her cheeks as she came, the sound of her heavy breathing as they recovered afterward, the sweet laughter.

Teddy was still smiling when his cell phone rang, and Jess's assistant Bee called to tell him that Jess was missing.

CHAPTER TWENTY-THREE – HOUSE OF CARDS

Los Angeles

JESS OPENED her eyes and groaned. Even in the faint light, it hurt her head, the pain inside her skull maddening. She blinked a couple of times as she orientated herself. She was tied to a chair, her hands were bound behind her back, her legs tied at the knees and ankle. In the dim light of the room she was in, she could tell it was some kind of wine cellar, a bank of bottles against three walls and on the fourth, she could see an open door leading to a stone staircase. The air was dank and musty, the only light coming from a bare bulb in the middle of the ceiling.

Jess looked around and gave a sharp intake of breath. The body of a middle-aged woman lay across the room, her throat cut, her eyes open and staring. Beside her, a man sat with his head in his hands, knees pulled up to his chest, a bloody knife on the floor beside him.

"Who are you?"

Somehow it wasn't a shock when the man looked up. Taran Googe, but he looked different. Wilder. Unhinged. She couldn't see from where she was, and her eyesight was compromised, but Jess would bet all the money in her checking account that Googe was high on… something.

Googe stared at her, then gestured at the dead woman. "*She* told me that no one would be home. That no one would see me bring you here. That I could enjoy myself with you before I killed you."

Jess felt adrenaline course through her system at his words. He was going to murder her? Taran Googe? God damn, she had underestimated him. Her eyes flicked to the dead woman. "Who is she? Why would she want me dead?"

Taran laughed without humor. "Not her. She's just the fucking housekeeper as far as I know." He scrambled to his feet, scooping the knife up and approaching her. Jess braced herself. Taran squatted in front of her. "Not her. Dorcas Prettyman."

Oh, God, no… "Why? Why would Dorcas want me dead?"

Taran smiled. "Besides that fact you're fucking her husband?"

"Ex-husband. And I can't believe Dorcas would hire

you of all people to kill me just for sleeping with her ex. She's setting you up, Taran."

Taran laughed. "I think not. Dorcas and I have a very close relationship. Very close." He leered at her. "And if you're a better fuck than Dorcas, then I don't know what to tell you. And anyways, it's not just the Teddy thing. She knows you know."

Jess frowned. "I... know?"

"About her kid. About her tainting the kid's milk."

Jess went cold. Please don't be right... but she knew she was. "She's poisoning her kid?"

Taran smirked. "Every wondered why she carries around so many bottles of eyedrops? They're all over her house. She puts them in the kid's cereal. I spent the night here once, saw her doing it. She knows I saw her, and so she told me another reason she wants rid of you is that. She figures she can get Teddy back if the kid is always sick."

Jess wanted to cry at that, not for herself, but for DJ. The cruelty of it. Dorcas Prettyman was even more evil than she had imagined. But that wouldn't help Jess now. She had to get out of here, so she could get to Teddy, to tell him, to save DJ's life. She flicked her eyes towards the dead woman. "You didn't have to kill her."

Taran smiled, and before he spoke again, he very carefully cut off all the buttons on Jess's shirt and pulled the fabric apart, exposing her. Jess felt cold air on her bare skin, and she gritted her teeth as Taran's fingers reached for the fly of her jeans. So this was what was going to happen, huh?

No way, buddy. He'll have to untie her legs if he wanted to... and then she would be able to kick, fight...

But he fanned out the fabric of the top of her jeans and did no more, confusing her. He was staring at her body. "I never thought I could kill someone. But today, I did. So really, I have nothing to lose by killing you, Jess. Nothing. I'll walk away from here."

"This isn't you, Taran." *Stay calm, don't panic.* "You're not a killer."

He motioned with the knife towards the dead woman. "But I am. She died quickly, but you won't. You won't at all, Jess. You shouldn't have called me *boy*."

Fuck... but she couldn't do anything as he held the knife against the skin of her belly. "Taran... Dorcas is setting you up. You killing me and her housekeeper... do you really think she will back you up? Give you money to escape the country? No way, baby. She'll spin this the way the way she needs to, that you acted alone, that you've been harassing her."

She saw the doubt in Googe's eyes as she spoke and grabbed onto that last vestige of hope. "This isn't you, Taran," she said again, gently. "You have to stop, otherwise it's not just me and that poor woman who loses. It's an eight-year-old kid, Taran. She'll kill her own kid to get her own way, and she'll feed you to the wolves to save herself."

"Shut up."

"I can't. I love that kid, and we need to save her. Think about it..."

"I said, shut up!" Taran's eyes were wild now, but Jess couldn't stop. She knew she was getting to him.

"Taran, listen to me..." Her words cut off with an agonized gasp as Taran drove the knife into her. Jess felt the searing agony shoot through her, and she closed her eyes. This was it... she was going to die, and the worst thing was that now, she couldn't save DJ.

Oh, Teddy... I'm sorry...

TEDDY TRIED NOT to let the panic take over. The police had come to the hospital to talk to him, and he'd peppered them with questions on Jess's whereabouts.

When Jess had failed to turn up to the courthouse for her client, her assistant Bee had called around trying to find her, but failing. She'd sent someone to the house, had called Massimo and India and Alex, but no one had seen her. After calling around everywhere, she'd called Teddy, and he'd gone down to the parking garage to find her car still there and blood on the ground.

He'd called the police immediately. When he went back upstairs, Dorcas came to him and made a show of comforting him. "Look, I have people, detectives on retainer. I can get them on it."

He didn't want her involved but at this point, he would do anything. Teddy wanted to go himself, go out into the city, drive to every place he had ever been with Jess to try to find her, but he had DJ to consider. This morning, after everything had begun, the doctor noted he thought his daughter was coming out of her coma, and so she could wake at any time. God, was this his choice? Solomon's choice? DJ or Jess?

He knew in his heart that Jess would tell him to stay with DJ, but it killed him to make that decision. After the police had talked to him, he went to take a moment alone, to think, to breathe. He stood in the stairwell, gazing out of the window over the city.

Where are you, my darling love? Please, please, be okay... Teddy knew it was probably futile, but he called her cell phone anyway, just to hear her sweet voice on her voicemail message. The police had told him Taran Googe was also missing, and he knew without a doubt, that he had Jess somewhere. They had underestimated his obsession with her, God damn it.

He went back to DJ's room, but before he could go in, DJ's doctor stopped him and asked him to step into his office. "Mr. Hood... I'm afraid I have some news that you might find distressing. We have already informed the police, but they are waiting until I have informed you before they act."

"I'm sorry, I have no idea what you're talking about."

"I began to have suspicions... we ran a battery of toxicology tests, and in particular, looking for certain chemicals found in everyday objects, things that would not normally raise suspicion. We found unusually high levels of a compound called tetrahydrozoline hydrochloride. At the levels we found in DJ's system, it can cause vomiting, high blood pressure, coma. Sound familiar?"

Teddy couldn't breathe. "What? How the hell would DJ get access to it?"

The doctor's expression was grim. "It's a common component of over-the-counter eye drops."

This time Teddy's knees gave way, and he sank into a chair. "What?"

"More than one of our staff have witnessed your ex-wife with these eyedrops, Mr. Hood. I checked her medical records. She's allergic to them. Why would she be carrying around eyedrops that she was allergic to?"

"Oh, no, no, no..." Teddy buried his head in his hands. Jess had been right all along. Dorcas was poisoning DJ, her own child. Jesus...

The doctor perched on the corner of his desk and looked at him sympathetically. "I'm so sorry, Mr. Hood. There's a name for this..."

"Munchausen's by proxy," Teddy said in a numb tone. "I've heard of it. Hell, I just thought Dorcas was milking the situation, not that she created it."

"It is a psychological disorder, but we still need to inform the police. They're waiting to make the arrest now."

Teddy looked up. His anger was past the raging point; now it was a white-hot heat burning deep in his soul. "I want to talk to her first."

The doctor looked unhappy but nodded. They walked back to her room, and the doctor spoke quietly to the police as Teddy pushed his way into DJ's room. Dorcas was sitting by her daughter's side, a supercilious look on her face. She smiled when she saw him. "Darling, is there any news about Jessica?"

Was there something triumphant in her eyes? Teddy's anger made it impossible to judge. "I know, Dorcas."

"Know what, darling?"

Teddy stared at her until she looked up and met his gaze. He saw her pale and quell in the face of his anger. "The eyedrops, Dorcas. The eyedrops you've been putting into our daughter's juice, her milk, her water. They cause all the symptoms DJ's been having. And they found it, Dorcas. In her blood."

"Don't be ridiculous. You're just upset about Jessica's abduction."

Teddy went very still. "Who said Jess was abducted?" He stepped towards his ex-wife, suddenly seeing the madness in her, the obsessive jealousy at its most horrifying. "What do you know about her disappearance, Dorcas? She knew, she suspected about you, and you knew it, right? What did you do to her?"

Dorcas stood, pushing the chair away from her. "Nothing! You're being ridiculous."

Teddy had her by her throat against the wall in a flash. "What did you do to DJ? What did you do to Jess?" He was yelling now, and he barely felt it when the police dragged him away from Dorcas. "She knows where Jess is, God damn it... she poisoned my daughter, now she knows where Jess has gone..."

It took a while for him to gather himself as they

arrested Dorcas and led her from the room. He felt mad, out of control... "Mr. Hood, breathe... we're looking into it. We're going to your ex-wife's house. We've had a report of a woman screaming."

"It's Jess... it's *Jess*..." Teddy kissed his daughter's head and yelled, "Look after her!" at the doctor and raced from the room. *I'm coming, Jess, I'm coming...*

24

CHAPTER TWENTY-FOUR – FADED

Los Angeles

SHE WAS LOSING TOO much blood from the stab wound, and Jess knew she had very little chance now. After stabbing her—just the once—Taran had backed off, sitting back on his haunches, staring at her blood pooling around her, around the chair. Jess felt light-headed, the pain nothing to the feeling of losing control. One good thing—if he'd nicked an artery or severed it, she'd be dead already.

So there was a chance, no matter how little. She tried to steady her breathing. "I forgive you for that, Taran. I forgive you. The drugs... did Dorcas give them to you?"

Taran nodded. He seemed in shock now, the effects of the drugs wearing off.

"I think she gave you something different than what you expected." God, she could taste her own blood. "This isn't you, Taran. You're not a killer."

"I'm not a killer..." He whispered it, but then he began to sob. "Oh God, oh God, oh God..."

Jess let him sob, then spoke quietly, kindly. "Taran... I'm dying. I'm going to bleed out. Could you untie me, so I can at least lie down?"

He nodded and came towards her. He cut her ties and helped her out of the chair. Jess found she could hardly move, her muscles not complying with her brain's instructions to run, fight. She tried to lay down, but then unexpectedly, Taran picked her up in his arms. "I'm sorry. I'll get you some help."

As they climbed the stairs and got into the main house, they heard the sirens. Taran put Jess down gently onto the couch in the living room. Her head whirled now with dizzying bright lights parking at the corner of her vision. Taran disappeared and came back with a clean towel. He pressed it against her wound. She met his gaze.

"I opened the gate for them and the front door. I'll take whatever they throw at me. I'm sorry, Jess."

It was such a turnaround that it too made her head spin, but she'd take it. "Tell them what she did to you. I'll... if I live, I'll speak up for you. Tell them you tried to save me at the end. Tell them Dorcas was to blame for everything. But Taran, promise me, first of all, you'll tell them about the eyedrops, about what Dorcas did. The priority is DJ... always DJ... *please*..."

She was fading now, but just before she passed out, she heard the sweetest sound she would ever hear in her life.

Teddy, calling her name over and over...

Los Angeles
Thirty-six hours later...

Jess opened her eyes to see the bright Los Angeles sun shining through the windows of her hospital room. Someone was holding her hand, and she looked down to see India, her face tearstained. "Indy?"

India looked up, her eyes full of surprise and delight... and she immediately burst into tears. Jess laughed and winced as the movement pulled on her stitches. "Indy, why are you crying? I'm okay."

India kissed her full on the mouth, still crying, and then ran out of the room, shouting for Teddy and Massimo. Jess laughed again, shaking her head. She was still hooked up to a blood bag, but she felt remarkably okay.

A second later, Massimo, Alex, and Lazlo, India's brother, came into the room and all of them hugged her—gingerly—and kissed her cheek. Jess was grateful for their love, but one question was in her mind. Where was Teddy?

India read her mind and smiled through her tears.

"He's just coming. He's just bringing someone eager to see you, too."

Then he was there, her love, her Teddy, looking more handsome than he'd ever had, all blue eyes and scruffy black hair and in his arms, smiling, her face flushed with health, was his daughter.

Jess gave a cry of joy and held her arms out, and Teddy, smiling, placed his daughter carefully on the bed next to Jess. Jess wrapped her arms around both of them, her own tears pouring down her cheeks, and hugged them tightly. "Oh, my DJ, my Teddy..." She kept repeating it over and over until the others chuckled. When she looked up, her friends had discreetly left the room, giving her time with her family.

And she knew, without a doubt now, this was her family. Her man, her girl. "I love you both so, so much... and I know I'm not your mommy, DJ, but I love you like you are my own. How are you feeling?"

DJ grinned at her, playing with the name tag on Jess's wrist. "Better, thank you. We'll all be better now, the doctor said. Daddy?"

Teddy couldn't take his eyes off Jess's face, and she flushed with pleasure at the love in his eyes. "Yes, sweetie?"

"Can I come live with you and Jess now?"

Jess laughed. "You'd better... yes?" She looked at Teddy, suddenly shy, but he nodded.

"Hell, yes."

Both Jess and DJ laughed at his cussing, and Teddy gathered them both in his arms. "We're a family now, right? And I promise both of you, we are going to be the happiest family in the world."

Jess kissed DJ's soft hair. "You bet your sweet ass we are," she said, grinning wickedly as DJ laughed at them both. DJ's arms snaked around Jess's neck, and Jess felt the young girl's soft, loving kiss on her cheek. It made her heart feel like it had swollen up to twice its size with the love she felt for this precious child. "I promise you," she whispered to DJ, "I will always, always keep you safe, my darling."

Teddy's face was full of emotion, and she looked up at him as DJ hugged her tightly. "Dorcas?" She mouthed at him and he nodded.

"She's been charged. She's going away from a long time." He nodded at DJ, who was watching them. "I'm not hiding this from DJ, so we can talk freely. Isn't that right, DJ?"

DJ nodded. "Daddy said I could still see Mommy if I want." She looked down at her tiny hands. "But I don't want to," she added in such a small voice that Jess's heart cracked.

She smoothed DJ's hair. "You won't have to do anything you don't want to, but listen, you know you can change your mind at any time, right, Teddy?"

"Absolutely. No one is going to make you do anything you don't want to do, not ever again."

DJ smiled, the relief obvious in her eyes. She looked between Jess and Teddy. "Daddy, are you going to marry Jessie?"

Jess flushed bright red, but Teddy grinned. "If she'll have me. This is not the proposal I planned, but to hell with it..." He shuffled from the bed and dropped to one knee.

"Daddy, wait." DJ pulled a plastic ring from her tiny finger and gave it to her father, who chuckled.

"Thank you, honey."

Jess and DJ laughed then, and as Jess felt breathless, Teddy took her hand. "Jessica Olden... right here, right now, I'm looking at the two loves of my life. The two people who I would walk through fire for. The two people whom I love more than life itself. I will try and try to be the best man for you both. DJ is my daughter, and now, Jessie, I ask you, humbly, to do me the honor of being my wife. Will you marry me?"

"Yes," Jess said without hesitation, and DJ yelled happily, cheering. Teddy got up and tried to slip the tiny ring onto Jess's finger. It fit—barely—in the top of her little finger and they all laughed.

"Daddy, I think you have to get a better ring," DJ ordered him bossily, which made them laugh again.

"I will," Teddy promised her, and he kissed DJ's forehead before pressing his lips to Jess's own, kissing her tenderly. "I love you so much."

"And I love you, baby. So, so much...forever..." and she kissed him again.

. . .

THREE DAYS LATER, Teddy proposed again, this time with a beautiful diamond, and Jess repeated her love for him and for DJ.

A week later, they were married.

Six months later, Jess formally adopted DJ as her daughter and knew her family was complete.

25

CHAPTER TWENTY-FIVE – ACROSS THE UNIVERSE

 *few months later...*

NEW YORK STATE

JESS PICKED DJ up and swung her around as they made their way down India and Massimo's long garden. "Oof," she said, setting her nine-year-old daughter down. "Either you're getting too big or I'm getting too old to do that."

DJ grinned at her. "Both?"

"Cheeky monkey!" Jess chased her around until they heard Teddy calling to them. He walked down to greet them and kissed Jess hello.

"You both look fantastic," he said, approving of their wedding outfits. It was India and Massimo's double wedding with their friends from Korea, Sun and Tae, and all three of the Hood family were excited to at last see their friends married.

They made their way to the flower-strewn guest area and found their seats in the front rows with Lazlo and Gabe, India's brothers. Jess excused herself and went to find India. She was in her room, giggling and getting ready with Sun, who looked so beautiful himself, that Jess wondered if she could have coped sharing her wedding with someone so otherworldly beautiful. But Sun was such a sweetheart that she knew she would have, and after all, her own wedding was very different: Teddy and DJ and her at City Hall, then a slap-up meal together on the beach outside their home. It had suited Jess and Teddy just fine.

"Hey cuties, you both look disgustingly beautiful," Jess mock-grimaced at then and grinned. "Is there anything I can do?"

India, stunning in her simple white dress, smiled at her friend. "No... we were just celebrating that we all survived... seems fitting you arriving just as we talked about what happened. We all survived."

"Bah, what happened to me doesn't compare, and why are we talking about *that* of all things today? Come on, gorgeous people, let's get you married."

. . .

THE WEDDING WAS SO beautiful that Jess even saw Gabe, India's hard-edged brother, wipe away a tear. India, Massimo, Sun, and his love Tae were married in a flash, and then the party began. DJ ran around with the other children in the party and enjoyed herself.

Jess saw Alex, still grieving for Coco and his child, finally smile at last, a genuine smile, and she hugged him and wished him every happiness. "I'll get there, Jessie," he said and then chuckled. "Right now I'm wondering why I'm not Korean."

Jess followed his gaze to the other members of Sun and Tae's band, all of them as handsome as the happy couple. "Hey, go for it, big guy."

"I'm old enough to be their father," Alex groaned. "When did I get so old?"

"You'll always be a catch, babe, even when you're sixty." She kissed his cheek and left him, laughing. She noticed a couple of India's male friends—around Alex's age—eyeing him appreciatively, and knew her friend wouldn't be lonely for long.

AFTER THE NEWLYWEDS had left for their honeymoon in Fiji, Teddy and Jess took DJ back to the hotel where they were staying, and after DJ was asleep, Teddy and Jess sat outside on the balcony and shared a bottle of champagne. "What a wonderful day," Jess sighed happily, tucking her head into the crook of Teddy's neck. He kissed her forehead.

"Every day will be as wonderful for all of us from now on, I promise."

Jess smiled up at him. "I believe you. Oh, hey, I forgot. I got you a present."

Teddy looked bemused. "You did? Is it your legs around my waist?"

"Oh, absolutely, but I got you another one, too. It's wrapped up, you just have to open it."

She didn't make any move to get up, though, and he shook his head. Finally she pointed to the buttons on her dress. "Unwrap."

"Ha." He put his champagne flute down and began to unbutton her dress, stroking each piece of exposed skin. When he got to her stomach, he saw it. Drawn in Sharpie was a small blob. Next to it, an arrow pointing to it, and then she had written "Hello, Daddy."

Teddy blinked, it taking a moment to sink in. Then he whooped loudly, making Jess both laugh and hush him. "You'll wake the rest of the hotel up."

"I don't care!"

He scooped her into his arms and carried her to their bedroom. "Oh my God! Jessie, really?"

"Really."

"How long have you known?" He was kissing her belly now, and pushing her dress from her shoulders at the same time. She laughed at his contorting her body in his eagerness to make love to her.

"Only a few days. I didn't want to overshadow the

wedding, plus I took about a hundred tests to make sure. But yes, we're going to have a baby, Teddy. Our baby. DJ is going to be a big sister."

He silenced her with his lips then, and they began to make love. His mouth moved down her body, trailing his lips along her jawline, then kissing the hollow of her throat.

Jess tangled her fingers in his dark hair as he made his way down her body, sucking at her nipples until they were almost unbearably sensitive and rock-hard, then his tongue traced the line down her stomach, circling her navel, dipping deep into the hollow of it.

Jess shivered with pleasure as he eased her panties off. "I want to taste you, too, baby."

They moved around so that she could take his rock-hard cock into her mouth. She trailed her tongue up and down the quivering shaft, hearing him groan as she felt him close his mouth over her clit.

Teddy nipped lightly at her clit with his teeth, making her moan then as the tension between them grew, they both began to move and moan with more fervor. Jess felt Teddy stiffen and he came, shooting into her mouth, and she eagerly swallowed him down as he drove her towards her own peak.

Her back arched up, and she cried out as she came, and she felt Teddy move, pulling out of her mouth and turning so he could gather her to him. His cock was already hardening again as they both panted for air, and for a long moment, Teddy gazed down at her, the love in his eyes almost overwhelming. There seemed to be no need for words between them at times like this, and Jess smiled up at him.

Teddy brushed his lips lightly against hers, once, twice, soft kisses that suited the tenderness of the moment and reflected the obvious joy in him. Jess smoothed her fingers over his face, marveling at the perfection of his features, wondering if their baby would look more like her or him. She hoped he or she would be as gorgeous as DJ was, the tomboy who looked like her dad with her bright blue eyes and dark hair. Jess took Teddy's hand and put it on her stomach, over their child, and kissed him, nodding at the question in his eyes.

Then he was animal again, hitching her legs around his waist and thrusting his hot, long cock deep inside her, harder and deeper until she was crying out again. "Oh, God, Teddy…. Teddy…"

Jess came hard, shuddering and shivering, completely losing herself in him and the moment. "God, I love you," Teddy gasped as he, too, climaxed, pumping semen deep inside her. Jess clung to him as they recovered.

"Stay inside for a while. I need you in me," she whispered to him, not wanting to break the connection, not now, not tonight as they caught their breath.

"I'll be with you forever," he told her, kissing her again so passionately it took her breath away.

"Promise?"

Teddy smiled down at her, his hand splayed over her belly again and nodded. "I promise."

Eight months later, their twin boys, Matthew and Mark, were born, and Teddy and Jess knew, at last, that their family was complete.

The End.

Did you like this book? Then you'll LOVE All of Me: A BDSM Romance (Their Secret Desire Book three)

All I wanted was to start over, somewhere quiet, somewhere I didn't have to be me.
Tiger Rose, Hollywood movie star.
She's someone I don't even recognize as me anymore.
And now I found my haven...
And found *him*...
Lazlo. He's the last person I should fall for. He's from the entertainment world too...
But that face, that body... and his good, good heart. I can't resist him...
But can I risk my new-found peace for him?
My body says *yes... yes...*

Yes...
But I'm scared to love again, scared to trust...
Can Lazlo break down the wall I've build around my heart?

Start Reading All of Me

SNEAK PEEK - CHAPTER ONE EVERYTHING CHANGES

Start Reading All of Me

He levelled the gun at her and she knew this was it. "I thought you loved me," she said in a calm voice. Only a slight quiver at the end gave away her heartbreak.

"I do," he nodded, his eyes soft, "but I have to do this."

She drew in a deep breath as he fired, then crumpled slowly as the bullet ripped through her abdomen. Her legs gave way and she sank to the floor.

He put down the gun and came to her, cradling her in his arms. She felt his tears drip down onto her face. "I'm sorry, I'm so sorry…"

"It doesn't matter," she said, her voice weakening as she bled out, "it's all over now."

"I love you," he said, beginning to sob, but she shook

her head.

"Love doesn't do this, my darling... Love doesn't do this." She gave one last shuddering gasp of pain, then went still.

He clutched her to him and gave a howl of bottomless grief.

"And cut! Good job, people." The director and his team clapped the actors, and Tiger opened her eyes and grinned up at Sifrido, her costar.

"Douchebag."

"Drama queen." He helped her up as they laughed and high-fived each other. Sifrido nudged her with his shoulder. "And lucky, too, to be finished early. So, what's next for you?"

"Hanging with my brother." Tiger smiled back at her friend and costar. She and Sifrido had worked on many movies together now and had been close from the start. She enjoyed spending time with him and his wife Lucy when they were in the same place, which was rare if they weren't working, and it was with half-regret now that she told Sifrido that she was going out of town. "Apollo is between jobs and wanting to spend some quality time with his big sister. So, we're going to the Olympics for a week with no internet, no cellphones. We bought a small cabin up there."

"Nice." Sifrido nodded approvingly. "Washington is one of my favorite places."

Tiger smiled at him. Sifrido's wife, Lucy, and his biological son Nicco, both taught at a college in Seattle.

"Then I have the Malevolence press junket for a month. First here, then London and on and on." She grimaced and Sifrido laughed.

"You're really not used to them by now?"

"I just don't like being around that many people for that long. Thank God Teddy will be there to make me laugh."

Tiger said goodbye to her friend and went to thank the director. Cosimo DeLuca was one of her favorite people, and he frequently cast Tiger in his movies. He had been responsible for her first break in the industry ten years ago, and she remained utterly loyal to him, even doing small cameos for free and for no credit if he needed it.

He looked tired now as she went to find him in his trailer. Biba, his gorgeous wife, was with him, and she greeted Tiger with a hug. "You were incredible as always, Tiggy."

Tiger smiled at them both. "I hate to do this, but I have to say goodbye for a while. But promise me, when we're all free, we'll meet up for dinner at least?"

Cosimo, a devastatingly handsome Italian in his late forties with bright green eyes and dark curly hair, grinned at her. "It's a date. Just let us know when you're free, Tig, and we'll make it happen. And thank you for this... Not every actress would come in for a part where they were killed off in the first act."

Tiger laughed. She looked down at her costume, covered in the corn syrup they used for fake blood. "Are you kidding? A great death scene? Give me more."

Biba chuckled. "Actors."

"Actors," greed Tiger with a nod. She bid them goodbye and went to her trailer. Peeling off her ruined dress, wrinkling her nose as the syrup stuck the fabric to her skin, she removed the small 'blood' bag taped to her skin by the props people and stepped into her shower.

She took her time, enjoying the hot water cascading down her skin. Drying herself, she took a critical look in the mirror. She had never been one of the skinny actresses; she refused to lose weight for any role that required her to be unhealthily thin, and she had retained her curves through hiking and swimming rather than dieting.

Her skin was porcelain, her hair a dark, dark brown and cut into a bob. Her large violet eyes and full mouth made her passionately sought after by beauty brands to be their spokesmodel, but that wasn't Tiger's scene. She earned enough from her movies to make her financially secure and she wasn't a spendthrift.

Tiger valued her privacy more than anything. At thirty-two, she and her younger brother Apollo had been on their own since Tiger was eighteen, their parents both dying of cancer just a few months apart. Tiger and Apollo had been devastated, but she had known she had to step up to the plate and care for her fourteen-year-old brother. She'd intended to go to college but had been scouted by an elite model agency and started to get jobs right away. Her extraordinarily photogenic features helped make her an overnight sensation, and when she was offered her first film role, Tiger found her true vocation.

She'd proved all the doubters wrong by putting in a supporting performance that attracted awards buzz, and she'd even taken home a few of them. Since then, she had been in demand, which had made life for her and Apollo a whole lot easier. Her brainiac brother was able to go to Harvard—something of which Tiger was envious—but she was able to pay his way easily, and he swore he would one day pay her back.

Apollo was her best friend, her buddy. With his light brown hair and green eyes, he was popular with the opposite sex, but it was his warm, kind, loving character that drew people to him. He was more outgoing than Tiger, and although she didn't like to admit it, Tiger had learned a lot about being social from her younger brother, and it helped her overcome her natural shyness.

Now she hurriedly dried her hair and shoved it up into a messy ponytail, leaving her face free of makeup. She donned old sweats to be comfortable for the flight from Los Angeles to Seattle and packed up her belongings. She never brought much to set, just her books, laptop, and precious photos of Apollo and her friends.

The flight to Seattle was mercifully quick, and as Tiger hurried through the Arrivals lounge, she scanned the crowd for Apollo. Soon enough, she saw her lanky brother, leaning nonchalantly against the wall at the far end of the hall. Tiger gave a whoop of joy and ran to him.

Apollo swept her up into a hug. "Oof, big sis."

"Ha ha, shut up." She punched his arm lightly as he

put her down, and he took her bag from her. "You look good, Pol."

"I know," he said cockily and grinned. "And looking forward to our trip. Can you even imagine what those trails are going to be like? I hope you're fit, sis."

Tiger made a face, then laughed. "Hey, as long as there's plenty of food."

"Always."

They got into Apollo's car and he pulled out of the parking lot. "So... what happened with David?"

Tiger rolled her eyes. David Bao was her very recent ex-boyfriend, a sensationally attractive Korean-American actor who had loved her and who she... liked. There was no other word for it; David had been more invested in their two-year relationship than she had been, and eventually Tiger had to admit to herself that it wasn't fair on David. He was perfect: kind, funny, gorgeous—the full package—but Tiger just couldn't give enough of herself to him.

When she broke up with him, David had been devastated but accepting. "Just promise me, you will try to love someone someday." He'd told her softly during their tear-filled breakup. "You're too special not to be with someone."

Tiger had promised him but she knew she had been lying. Something was broken inside of her, she thought, that she couldn't trust enough to love, to give herself over to someone, and what was frustrating was that she didn't have any clue as to why. She hadn't been abused as a child or assaulted as an adult. Yes, she'd put up with her fair share of harassment and inappropriate casting couch proposals over the years, but she'd maintained a reputation for never being one of those actors, someone who would sleep around for parts.

She would also speak openly about that side of her craft in interviews, naming the worst offenders. It had cost her roles, sure, but it had also increased industry respect for her.

Now, as Apollo drove back to his apartment in the city, she grinned at her brother. "Not much to tell. He's doing okay, as far as I know."

"And you?"

"You know me."

Apollo's mouth set into a hard line, and Tiger was surprised to see him shake his head. "What's up with you?"

"Tigs... David was a good one."

"I know, but at the end of the day..."

"You couldn't let yourself love him."

Damn, Apollo knew her too well. Tiger looked away, out of the window. "It is what it is, Pol."

"You're thirty-two, Tigs. Isn't it time you figured this shit out? Why does this happen all the time?"

"Just leave it alone, Pol. I'm happy being single."

"And I'm all for that... but I don't think it's just a case of you liking your own company. There's a block there and I cannot figure for the life of me what it is."

"Seriously, why are you asking me this now? I thought we were here to enjoy a vacation together..."

"I met someone."

Tiger's eyebrows shot up and she saw that there were two spots of pink high on her brother's cheeks. "You did? That's wonderful."

Apollo nodded and couldn't help the smile breaking across his face. "She's wonderful. Nell. She's a postgraduate at college."

"Cute?"

"Beautiful. All dark hair and dark eyes and the longest legs you'll ever see."

Tiger smiled at the love in her brother's voice. "How long have you been seeing her?"

"Six months."

Tiger was shocked. "Six months? How come you haven't mentioned her before?"

Apollo was silent for a few moments as he concentrated on his driving. "Tig... she's pregnant. Three months."

Chapter Two – You Say

Tiger gaped at him. "What?"

Apollo nodded. "And, believe it or not... it was planned. Tigs... Nell and I... we're getting married. Soon."

Tiger was devastated. "Why did you keep this all from me? Did you think I wouldn't support you?"

"I know you would have, I know. Except... sometimes, you still think of me as a fourteen-year-old, and just sometimes you can be a bit..."

"What?" Tiger felt hurt, shockingly so. They had

always been so close and now what? Apollo didn't need her anymore?

"Smothering. No, that's not right. Overprotective. Especially with my girlfriends."

"If you're talking about Liz, that's because she was an evil demon from hell."

Apollo grinned then. "In that case, you are correct, but sometimes, just you being who you are, Tiger Rose, can be intimidating for them. Not that Nell will be, but I didn't know that at the start of us. So, I kept it from you." He suddenly pulled the car over into a parking lot and switched off the ignition. He turned to look at her. "Don't get me wrong, Tigs. I adore you, I love you, and you are the best thing in the world. But you paid for everything, you gave me everything, and now I need to... God, I don't know. This needs to be mine, you get me?"

"I get it." But she didn't. She looked away, out of the window, blinking back tears. Apollo felt overshadowed by her? God damn it. She'd tried not to let that happen and besides... "Listen, you didn't get into Harvard because of me, Pol, you did that on your own."

He smiled kindly at her. "With your money, Tigs. I'm sure the fact I had the funding in place helped immeasurably with the offer of a place."

Alright, he had her there. But Tiger sighed. "Do I at least get to meet her?"

"After our vacation. When we come back to Seattle. She's spending the week with her folks in New Orleans while we're away; she didn't want to crash our vacay."

"That's thoughtful." Tiger shook her head. "Pregnant?"

Apollo nodded and she could see the joy in his eyes. "Honestly, Tigs, I never knew I wanted kids until I met Nell. She's the one, you know?"

But Tiger didn't know, and her heart ripped open with loneliness. She had known, of course, this day would come, when their little family unit would be invaded by someone else…

…invaded. What the hell is wrong with you, woman? Invaded. Tiger pulled herself together and smiled at her brother. "I'm delighted for you, Pol. Really."

He shot her a sideways look and a grin. "Nice try, sis."

"I mean it."

He patted her hand. "Thank you. Now, let's talk vacay."

They spent the night in the city. In the morning, Tiger padded into the kitchen to see Apollo watching the television news intently. He turned to her with troubled eyes. "Did you hear?" He nodded at the screen. "India Blue is in the hospital."

Tiger's eyebrows shot up. "Oh, no…"

Massimo Verdi, one of Tiger's friends in the business, had been seeing India Blue for a while, and Tiger had been on a double date with them a few months back. She'd like India very much. "What happened?"

"She was abducted. They found her this morning with serious stab wounds."

"Jesus."

Tiger sat down and watched alongside Apollo as the

report showed a very distressed Massimo arriving at the hospital along accompanied by a very tall, handsome man who looked stressed out, dark circles under his navy-blue eyes.

"Who's that?"

"I think it must be Lazlo Schuler, India's kind-of brother. It's complicated." Tiger had never met India's family, but she'd heard of Lazlo. He was India's manager and a brilliant one at that. But he looked devastated now, and Tiger's heart went out to him. "Poor things. I must send flowers to Massimo before we leave."

In the car on the way to the Olympic Mountains, Tiger couldn't stop thinking about Massimo and India. She knew part of her problem with never allowing anyone to love her was exactly this: the fear of the pain of loss. When their parents had died, it had been such an overwhelming, all-encompassing shock. An ordinary Saturday. Her mom and dad going to Walmart to pick up the weekly groceries. A logging truck with an exhausted driver turning onto the road, not seeing their small Volvo car traveling along the same stretch. It had been all over in a second, the police told them, their parents barely even realized what had been happening.

The pain was unimaginable, and when the then-eighteen-year-old Tiger had to identify the remains—because 'remains' were all that was left of her Mom and Dad—it seared the experience into her psyche. No. She had Apollo and that's all she needed.

One person to worry about constantly. One person to be scared of losing.

One to be overprotective of. Damn it. Look at Massimo and India. He was close to losing India in the worst way possible, and yet he showed up, he was there, he loved her regardless.

Her brother was right. It wasn't healthy, it wasn't sustainable, and now he had proved it. There would be a new life, her niece, that she would worry over.

And the woman her brother loved. Tiger trusted Apollo enough now to know that if he had made this commitment, then Nell was the one. A good person. A great person.

"You're right, Pol," she said softly as she drove and he turned to her.

"What?"

She smiled at him. "It is time."

"For?"

Tiger's grin widened and she nodded. "It is time for me to trust to love."

"Finally."

And they both laughed.

Chapter Three - Smithereens

One month later...

The press junket for her latest movie to be released had been long and arduous, but finally it was coming to an end. The last interviews were in New York at a Manhattan hotel, and Tiger found being interviewed in a small hotel room uncomfortable and trying, especially when she was asked the same questions over and over.

Thankfully, for the last interviews, she would be paired with her costar Teddy Hood. Teddy was going through a painful divorce, but he'd still stayed professional and cheerful throughout, doing his job, fulfilling his contract despite his woes. He confided to Tiger after each day that his smile felt false, that he felt as if he were playing a role, but hey, he said, "That's what I'm paid to do."

"You can always talk to me, Teddy," Tiger told him, kindly. "Anytime."

For herself, Tiger was looking forward to getting home to Seattle to finally meet Nell. They hadn't been able to make the meeting work before Tiger had to work, but this weekend was the time. She was nervous, but thanks to Apollo's machinations, she and Nell had at least talked over Facetime a couple of times, albeit casually.

Tiger decided to call Apollo now, between interviews. She'd just finished with a creep from a British tabloid, Grant Waller, whom she had never liked. The way his eyes roamed over her body, the way he always, always, asked her about her underwear, for chrissakes. The film had been a comic book-based superhero movie, and Tiger played one of the main heroes, clad in a tight leather suit. She'd played the role a couple of times now, and each time, Waller had asked her about what she wore under the suit. Tiger had been gracious and humorous at first, but this time, she had snapped back at him.

"How about we talk about your underwear, Mr. Waller? You seem to have a fixation with it, after all."

Grant Waller had smiled what he obviously thought was a charming smile, but it looked to Tiger like the grin of a snake. "I'm not the one on public show."

"Public show? Funny, I thought I was fully dressed throughout. Tell me, Mr. Waller, have you a mother? A sister?"

His smile had faltered a little. "Yes, why?"

"How would you feel about someone continually asking about their underwear?" She fixed him with an ice-cold stare and felt victorious when he'd backed off and asked another question. The interview limped on for another few minutes before the studio rep had called time. She hadn't bothered to shake Waller's hand afterward. Asshole.

Tiger talked to the rep for a few minutes, then excused herself to the hotel corridor to make a call.

"Hey, sis."

"Hey, loser. How's it going?"

Apollo laughed. "Since you last asked about two hours ago? We're doing good. We've got everything ready for your visit... or should I say, Nell has been tidying everything up fifty-five billion times because she's scared."

Tiger chuckled as she heard Nell in the background, protesting that Apollo was busting her. "Hey, tell Nell not to worry. When we're all together, I'll help her get her revenge on you."

"I will not tell her that," Apollo laughed, "Hey, listen, I—"

Tiger never knew what Apollo was about to say, because something, someone grabbed her from behind, and she dropped her phone. She was slammed full force into the wall of the corridor, and she felt hot breath on her ear. "Fucking stuck-up bitch," Grant Waller growled, his hands burrowing under her skirt, "Let's see how much of a whore you really are..."

Tiger struggled with him, crying out before he clamped his hand over her mouth. No. No, this wasn't going to happen...

But his strength was too much for her, and for the next few minutes, Tiger could only cry as Waller assaulted her. Only when he attempted to kiss her did she get an advantage, biting down on his bottom lip hard. She tasted blood as he screamed and pushed her away, slapping her around the face hard enough to knock her down. Tiger slumped to the ground as Waller walked away, wiping his mouth.

For a few long moments, all Tiger could hear was her own heavy breathing. She felt numb, shocked into incomprehension about what had just happened to her. Then, moving like an automaton, she stood shakily and straightened out her dress, her hair, wiped her mouth.

She checked her watch. Her final interview was happening right now. She walked to the designated room, barely acknowledging the studio reps or even Teddy, who shot her a concerned look as she sat down next to him.

"Hey, are you okay?"

Tiger looked at him blankly, not seeing him. The journalist was shown in and sat down and began to ask his questions. Somewhere inside her wrecked mind, Tiger knew she should be talking, but she couldn't form the words, couldn't understand plain English.

Suddenly Teddy stopped the interview and turned to her. "Seriously, this is off the record," he added to the journalist, who was looking equally concerned. She nodded, her eyes on Tiger. Teddy held Tiger's hands. "Tiger... honey, you're not okay, are you?"

She stared blankly at him and the felt something wet drip onto her neck.

"Jesus, you're bleeding..." Teddy looked at the reps, one of which quickly got on her cell phone to call for help.

Teddy pulled off his overshirt and pressed it to Tiger's head. "Honey, what happened? What happened?"

Finally, the dam broke inside of her, and she spoke, only in a whisper, but to her it sounded like a scream. "No... no, I'm not alright... I'm not alright at all..."

The movie's director stood at the podium with one of the studio lawyers and held his hand up for silence. The congregated press gaggle silenced. The director nodded.

"As you know, the press interviews scheduled for this afternoon were cancelled at short notice due to an incident. We can now confirm details of that incident. At precisely three-ten p.m., a beloved cast member was violently and sexually assaulted by a member of the tabloid press."

A furor broke out amongst the journalists, but the director wasn't finished. "This is unacceptable and horrifying. An arrest has been made, and we will be pressing charges against that journalist. The incident, while not witnessed by anyone in person, was captured on the hotel security cameras and was audibly witnessed by one of the cast member's family. We want to ask you, out of respect, not to try and speculate which cast member was the victim of this horrific attack nor invade their or their family's privacy."

"Can you confirm whether the cast member was male or female?" A question from the back.

The director glared at the whole pack. "What did I just say? The cast member is being cared for, and you will not invade his or her privacy. We will update you on the case when we have more."

Tiger watched the news conference dispassionately from her hospital bed. Along the bottom of the screen ran the words, 'Backslash Studios abruptly cancels press interviews in wake of serious 'incident.' Police have made arrest. Man charged with serious sexual offenses and assault.'

That was her they were talking about. She felt numb, almost paralyzed. Apollo had been frantic, hearing her being attacked, and the police had told her they were flying both Apollo and Nell out to be with Tiger.

Tiger closed her eyes. There were so many people

around her now that she felt she couldn't breathe. Grant Waller had been arrested, and she had been brought here where a laceration on her hairline was treated. Bruises were forming all over her body, but she couldn't feel the physical pain of them.

She waited until the others in her room were distracted before slipping out. She just needed a few minutes, just a few minutes peace to get her head together, and here, in this hospital, she felt safe enough to be alone.

She found a stairwell and curled up in a corner near a window. She heard a door well below her open but didn't hear anyone approach. It wasn't until someone far below her began to talk that she realized someone else was hiding out here, too.

"Jess? Jessie..." A man began to cry quietly, and the heartbreak in his voice made her eyes fill with tears. "It's okay. India's okay... it's just... I needed to talk to someone. I'm sorry if I've filled up your voicemail, I don't want to intrude. I just... Massi is so destroyed by this that I don't feel I can fall apart. Gabe is... Gabe. India's awake and she's trying to make jokes all of the time, but... I'm a wreck, Jessie." He laughed softly. "God, do me a favor, would you delete this? I'm just rambling like an idiot, but you're the only one I can share with. Everyone needs me, Jessie and... God, I'm sorry. Ignore me. I love you. I'll call you later."

Tiger heard him flicked his phone off, then heard the door open. "Mr. Schuler?"

"Yes?"

"Ms. Blue is asking for you."

"Of course."

The door squeaked again, and then Tiger knew she was alone in the stairwell. Lazlo Schuler. He sounded as wrecked as she felt right now. Tiger wondered if, like her, all he wanted to do was run away, leave everything and everyone behind, cocoon herself away from all the hurt and the pain in the world.

Because that was all she wanted to do now. The studio had released her from performing the rest of her public relation commitments, probably worried about being sued out the wazoo for not protecting her. So, she was going home, back to Washington, but not to Seattle. She knew exactly where she was going to go, somewhere no one would find her in a hurry: the small house she'd bought quietly a few years back to be a bolt hole. It would be perfect for her now. Apollo didn't need her in Seattle; he had Nell and the baby.

It was time for Tiger to finally be truly on her own.

Chapter Four - Tomorrow

Three years later...

The Island, San Juan Islands, Washington State

Lazlo Schuler pulled his car off the ferry boat and onto the island. The trip from Seattle had taken longer than he had expected, and he wondered now how wise it had been to drive rather than catch a plane and rent a car.

Luckily for him, the house he had rented for the next month wasn't far from the ferry port and soon he was inside, waiting for the realtor to leave him alone.

That was why he was here, after all. To be alone.

Lazlo Schuler was tired. No, more than tired; he simply had nothing left in him. In the last few years, he'd almost lost his beloved sister, India Blue, for the second time, and their adored Korean friend to a psychopathic killer, almost lost another to a vengeful ex-wife, and had lost his close friend Coco to an unexpected pregnancy complication. He was tired of loss, of grieving.

And he was tired of work. He managed not only his sister's career but others in the entertainment business, and most of them demanded more time than he could give.

But not India. He would work twenty-four-seven for his adopted sister, but it was she who sat him down two weeks ago and had gently told him she was worried.

He had gaped at her. "Indy... you're worried about me?"

She nodded, her dark eyes full of love and concern. "For a long time now. You've been our rock, all of us. With what happened to Sun and me, for losing Coco, and what's just happened to Jess, you've been there for all of us."

"That's my job."

"But you never, ever ask us for anything," India said, a note of frustration creeping into her soft voice.

"I don't need anything, bubba. Now that you're safe, Jess is safe, I have no worries."

But even as he'd said it, he knew he wasn't convincing

India because he knew it wasn't true. He wasn't doing okay, not at all. Sleep evaded him every night and to distract himself from the nightmares that plagued him, he would work. The clients who weren't personal friends were delighted, of course, but Lazlo was exhausted.

The final straw came when India played a curveball, and Lazlo came home one day to find his best friend, Alex Rogers, waiting for him.

Alex had been AWOL for a couple of years, ever since Coco Conrad, his roommate and the mother of his unborn child had died unexpectedly. Alex had been beyond grief and had disappeared back to his family in Canada. None of them ever thought they would see him again.

"But India called me and begged to come," he told Lazlo that evening. "Because she's scared out of her mind for you, Laz. Don't forget Indy knows the signs of a breakdown; she had that with Massi, and she got him through it. She sees the same signs with you, but she says you won't give anything away."

Alex talked to him over the next few days and convinced Lazlo to take a break. "Listen, I'll take over for you while you're on sabbatical. I'm not trying to steal your clients, but I need something to do. Hanging out with my family has been what I needed, but I want to get back to work. I'll even do it for free. It's not like I can't afford to. I'll just be a placeholder."

Lazlo trusted Alex at his word and after that evening, he had slept better than he had in years. He knew he needed to get away, but he was still too loathe to leave the country in case India needed him. She rolled her eyes, but as they talked about various locations, it was India who had suggested Washington.

"Remember when we went on that shindig with Quartet? We all stayed in that hotel on San Juan Island? It was bliss and well out of the way, but not isolated. Those islands, man, that would be prefect."

Lazlo had agreed, and so now as he bid the realtor to his rental goodbye, he closed the door and went into the living room. He'd rented the place furnished because he didn't want the hassle of being in an empty house—he was there to chill, after all.

In the corner of the living room sat a few boxes he'd had shipped: mostly books he'd been meaning to read for a while. He retrieved his laptop from his bag and flicked it on, making himself a cup of coffee while he waited for it to boot up. He couldn't resist checking his emails but laughed aloud when he saw twenty emails from India, all of them reading the same thing.

Don't you dare, Schuler. Your out-of-office is on and I have spies EVERYWHERE.

Lazlo grinned and replied to one of them with:

You are scary, but I love you. I promise, no work, just play. Laz.

As evening fell over the island, Lazlo walked around the little neighborhood. There was a pathway down to the beach, and he went down to it, watching the sunset, scanning the water for any orca sightings.

He was about to turn around when he saw a figure further down the beach, a woman walking a dog. He looked away, not wanting her to feel threatened at all by a lone man staring at her, but her dog clearly had other ideas. He skittered up to Lazlo, yapping happily and jumping up for a fuss. Lazlo grinned and bent to stroke the black-and-tan spaniel. "Hey, boy."

The dog's owner hurried up to them looking harassed. "I'm so sorry."

"It's no problem." He looked at the woman curiously. Even though the sun was dipping below the horizon, she wore sunglasses, and her hair, long, almost to her waist, was a deep almost-black. There was something vaguely familiar about her, but he didn't want to intrude on her privacy.

She clipped her dog's leash onto his collar and nodded politely at Lazlo before turning around. Lazlo in turn walked back to the pathway that led to his street and went home. It was nagging at him who the woman reminded him of—she couldn't be more than thirty, surely? What he had seen of her face was lovely: the sweet flush of pink on her cheeks, the full mouth.

Lazlo chuckled to himself. He hadn't come here to find a woman, but maybe, actually, it wasn't a bad idea to get back out in the game. Nothing heavy, nothing that would require a commitment. But fun. Some fun.

That was a word he hadn't applied to himself in way, way too long.

Tiger let Fizz off of his leash, casting a mock-stern glance at her dog. "What have I told you about jumping up, dude?"

Fizz, his mouth open in a wide doggy grin, panted at her, his eyes hopeful. Tiger rolled her eyes and dug a treat out for him from her pocket. "Not that you deserve it."

Fizz, satisfied, trotted away to his basket and flopped with a sigh into it. He was asleep even before Tiger had finished taking off her coat. Filling a kettle, Tiger set it to heat on the stove and found a clean mug, grabbing a tea bag from the little box. This was her little ritual. Walk the dog on the beach until the sun went down, a cup of herbal tea, a square of dark chocolate and a half hour of silence, sitting out on her deck, no matter how cold she got. Tiger preferred the fall, which it was now, when there were still warm days, but when the sun set, there was a bite to the air that she loved. It felt fresh, cleansing.

This whole island had been the best balm to her broken soul. The last two years, living here in virtual anonymity had been the relief she had needed after the trial of Grant Waller had dragged up the assault over and over in the press. Tiger had utterly bonded with Apollo's Nell after the woman had swept in like an avenging angel and taken care of both Tiger and her shocked, angry brother and kept them on an even keel.

Tiger had come to live with them for a few months, then when the furor had died down, she bought a place up here in the San Juan islands, far enough away that she didn't feel she was crowding her brother and his love, but close enough to travel to Seattle if they needed her. When her niece was born, Tiger fell in love straight away. Little Daisy was the light of her life, and she had found being with her made Tiger question more than anything if she really wanted to shut herself away or if there was something more.

And, she had to admit, she had been feeling the loneliness lately. Fizz helped; she'd rescued the dog from a local shelter a year ago and had never regretted it for a moment. Fizz was a bundle of fluffy love who was never but completely happy to see her and asked nothing but love—and food—in return. Fizz slept next to her in bed and woke her every morning with a gentle nudge of her muzzle and a tentative lick.

Tiger was also getting bored. She'd spent the last two years away from acting, catching up with all the other things she wanted to do in life, learning to play the piano, trying her hand at writing, blogging (under an assumed name, of course), and even taking a few evening classes in various topics. But during the day, she was slowly losing the need to be undercover. No one, so far as she knew, had recognized her. Her bobbed hair was long and wavy now and back to its natural color after years of being dyed and bleached and wrecked by different roles. She wore very little makeup, and because her screen persona had been very screen siren-esque and old film star-style, her natural look was so entirely different that she had started to relax around other people.

She had one coffee shop she was a regular at now, and

the owner, a sweet woman around her same age, often stopped to chat with her. Tiger only knew her as Sarah, and she'd told Sarah her name was Tig. There was no hint of recognition in the other woman's eyes, and Tiger slowly became more comfortable with the other woman and thought she may have found a new friend. It was a nice thought.

The next morning, she took Fizz and walked to the small main street and into her coffee house. Sarah looked up from behind the bar and smiled. "Hey, hello. I was wondering if I'd see you today."

Tiger grinned. "I'm like clockwork. And besides, Fizz wants to see his auntie."

Sarah adored the small dog and came to fuss him now. "Listen, I was hoping I'd see you. Can you sit and talk for a little while?"

Tiger was surprised. "Of course."

"Tea's on the house." Sarah went to serve a customer, then brought two steaming cups of Earl Grey tea over to a table. Tiger thanked her.

Sarah smiled. "I have ulterior motives. Now, I'm going to have to overstep here, but I need to ask you something."

Tiger's heart sank but she nodded anyway. She liked Sarah, and she wouldn't lie if Sarah questioned her about her true identity.

Sarah drew in a nervous breath. "Now, not that I don't love seeing you every day, but I'm assuming since you're here when most other people are at work, you don't?"

Tiger grinned, relieved. "Not at the moment. I'm on a sabbatical that somehow stretched into a couple of years. Why do you ask?"

"Because, if you don't think I'm being out of line, I wondered if you needed a part-time job? It's just my barista Bella is off to college at Northwestern soon, and I thought I had a replacement lined up, but she called last night and told me she'd been headhunted by someone else." Sarah sighed, smiling shyly at Tiger. "You can say no, and I won't be at all offended. It's just, I like you, and I think we could have fun working together."

"I don't have any experience in barist...ing—is that the word?" Tiger laughed. "But I'd be happy to help, happy to learn."

Sarah's eyes opened wide. "Really?"

"Really. I had been thinking about what to do next, and I love this place." She looked down at Fizz, laying patiently at her feet. "Can I bring Fizz to work with me?"

"Of course!" Sarah looked close to tears, smiling widely. "God, I'm so happy, Tigs."

Tiger felt a wave of fondness for the other woman and her use of her old nickname. She clearly didn't realize who Tiger was. Who I used to be, Tiger thought now, nodding to herself. That was a million miles away, a million years. "I'm glad... hey, I'm excited about it. When do you want me to start?"

"Anytime in the next two weeks if that's at all possible. That's how long I still have Bella and between us, we can train you."

Tiger picked up her cup and clinked it against Sarah's. "Let's drink to it... boss."

Sarah laughed. "Ha. I like to think of it more as a partnership. Thank you, Tigs."

Tiger was still smiling when she got home, and as she walked in, her cell phone rang. She saw it was Apollo calling her and she smiled. "Hey, bro, you called just at the right time. Guess who got a job?"

Apollo was silent for a beat too long, and suddenly Tiger sensed his tension. "What? What is it? Is it Daisy? Is it Nell?"

She heard her brother draw in a deep breath. "No, darling," he said gently. "No, we're all fine, don't worry. Tigs... it's Grant Waller."

"What about him?"

"Oh, Tigs... he's out of jail. They let him out early."

Start Reading All of Me

https://books2read.com/u/bO6ppK

If you want to read the entire Their Secret Desire Series at a discount, you can get the complete box set by clicking here.

Their Secret Desire: Billionaire Romance

https://books2read.com/u/3RKkQn

www.ingramcontent.com/pod-product-compliance
Lightning Source LLC
LaVergne TN
LVHW021655060526
838200LV00050B/2360